I've travelled the world twice over,
Met the famous: saints and sinners,
Poets and artists, kings and queens,
Old stars and hopeful beginners,
I've been where no-one's been before,
Learned secrets from writers and cooks
All with one library ticket
To the wonderful world of books.

HEROES NO MORE

Each year, three survivors of a Lancaster bomber crew of World War Two—along with their wives—attend a re-union in a Lancashire hotel. They are ageing now. As one says, "We are in our prime, except for age, there is nothing wrong with us". As they eat and drink their way through the long "re-union", tension mounts, and for some time is running out at last. This marvellous evocation of old days and new conflicts comes to its climax in a stunning sequence of shocks and surprises.

Books by John Wainwright
in the Ulverscroft Large Print Series:

DUTY ELSEWHERE
LANDSCAPE WITH VIOLENCE
MAN OF LAW
BLAYDE, R.I.P.
SPIRAL STAIRCASE
CUL-DE-SAC
THE DISTAFF FACTOR
HEROES NO MORE

JOHN WAINWRIGHT

HEROES NO MORE

Complete and Unabridged

ULVERSCROFT
Leicester

First published in Great Britain in 1983 by
Macmillan London Ltd.

First Large Print Edition
published November 1985
by arrangement with
Macmillan London Ltd.

British Library CIP Data

Wainwright John, *1921–*
Heroes no more.—Large print ed.—
Ulverscroft large print series: mystery
I. Title
823′.914[F] PR6073.A354

ISBN 0-7089-1383-0

Published by
F. A. Thorpe (Publishing) Ltd.
Anstey, Leicestershire
Set by Rowland Phototypesetting Ltd.
Bury St. Edmunds, Suffolk
Printed and bound in Great Britain by
T. J. Press (Padstow) Ltd., Padstow, Cornwall

Show me a hero and I will write you a tragedy.

F. Scott Fitzgerald
Notebooks, C

1

The Hotel

THE Cave Hotel, Lytham St. Annes. Ask around. Ask any hotelier, any restaurateur in the whole Fylde area. The honest ones won't hesitate, those with a personal axe to grind might hum and haw a little but, if pressed, they'll make reluctant admission. The best hotel for fifty miles around. Easily. Forget Blackpool, forget Morecambe, forget Southport. Forget every other hotel or eating establishment within even moderate driving distance. The Cave tops the lot and has the stars and the clientele to prove it.

Not large. The Cave refuses to even hint at vulgarity. It is a modest sixty-roomer, but each room has its own en-suite bathroom, complete with toilet, bath, needle-shower, bidet, etc. and each bedroom has its adjoining, compact lounge, complete with French windows leading to a tiny but adequate balcony overlooking the sea. You book a 'room' at The Cave and you get three rooms; bedroom, bathroom and lounge. Nobody tells you this; it is assumed that any person of discretion knows The Cave and that the tariff covers (among other things) over-the-odds salaries to an average of six members of staff whose task it is to pander to the comfort of each guest twenty-four hours a day.

Bed linen and towels are changed each day. Table linen is used once, then replaced and sent to the hotel laundry. The slightest chip or mark on glass or china, and the offending piece is thrown away. Dirt and even the ghost of grubbiness is barred. Each room (even each bathroom) has its own carefully selected colour scheme, complete with appropriate furnishing and drapes. All air entering the hotel is "conditioned", all windows are double-glazed and every radiator has its own thermostat which can be set as individual guests require. The dining room is a poem of green and gold. The bar is cunningly planned to give the appearance of a series of redwood-walled rooms, each large enough to hold the average group of social drinkers, yet small enough to create an atmosphere of cosy confidentiality. The sun lounge is long enough, and large enough, to hold all guests, if necessary, and with ample room to spare; the deep armchairs and strategically placed knee-high tables give both comfort and a magnificent view through the floor-to-ceiling windows of the hotel gardens, the promenade, Lytham Green and, beyond the green, the changing reflections on the surface of the Irish Sea.

The man in the lightweight, sand-coloured suit sprawled even deeper into the soft upholstery of one of the armchairs, glanced at his wrist-watch and frowned.

"If they aren't here soon, I'll have to have a word with somebody. Make the dinner-booking an hour later."

His wife made a soft, grunting noise of agreement—or perhaps it was disagreement—from the companion armchair and refused to move her concentration from the Agatha Christie paperback.

There is little need to describe them, other than that they were late-middle-aged, approaching elderly. They were at least moderately affluent—otherwise they wouldn't have been staying at The Cave—

and it showed in their clothes, the man's thickness at the waist and his wife's blue-rinsed hair and carefully corseted figure.

Their names were James and Emily Bathurst.

2

The Motorway

EVEN those who don't like it—even those who detest all motorways—must admit (albeit reluctantly) that the M6 is a very impressive piece of civil engineering. It leaves the M1 at junction nineteen, arrows across the Black Country through the northern outskirts of Coventry, into the heart of Birmingham and, north of West Bromwich, takes over from the M5. From there it races north, never too far from the west coast, to Carlisle and beyond. A great, drunken "L" which imposes itself on any road map of England, it is in parts old and in constant need of repair; those who originally planned it projected an estimated traffic-flow and were miles out in their estimate. It feeds heavy goods vehicles to and from the industrial Midlands and the west coast ports, and holiday-makers to a string of resorts and the Lake District. It is never silent. Never "quiet". Red-and-white cones, flickering amber lights and traffic-direction signs peculiar to motorway repair gangs make a mockery of the triple-lane carriageway with metronomic regularity and the tail-backs build up, engines over-heat and tempers are frayed.

The Cortina had a stretch of comparatively open road ahead, and the driver swung into the overtaking lane and eased the accelerator down until the needle flickered past the 80 mark.

He muttered, "Dammit, we're going to be late."

The woman alongside him said, "Is that important?"

"Yes, it's important. ETA was six o'clock, and we've Preston ahead of us yet."

"ETA?"

"Skip it." He stared ahead and concentrated on fast driving.

The man was of the age of Bathurst (give or take a year or two) but slimmer, and giving the impression of being a little frayed at the edges; a regular off-the-peg-suit man who, when he bought cigarettes, asked if anything was "on offer". Not poor, but careful. A man who, if he didn't actually count the pennies, kept a keen eye on the pounds. And yet, the impression was of a man with a touch of vanity. The careful trim of the hair with its deliberately cultivated "wings" of near-white grey. The neat moustache whose edge was razor-sharp and immaculately shaped. There was an air of "con" there, but without the false, plastic sheen of the genuine confidence trickster: until you made careful examination of the eyes.

At first glance they appeared to be eyes without expression; cold, dead eyes. But look hard and in their depths there was pain. Not physical pain, but pain of the soul; the pain brought about by mental anguish as if, all his life, he'd gutted himself and never received the credit of his worth; the pain of a man who, throughout every race, leads the field but never breasts the finishing tape first.

The woman was his wife, and his junior by at least twenty years. A certain bovine quality—the hint of mild gormlessness—spoiled what could have been a handsome enough face. Handsome, not beautiful. Not even pretty. The bones were too heavy for beauty. The chin was a few sizes too large.

And yet there was about her a strange air of *cleanliness*. The mousey hair had been brushed regularly until it shone with health. There was an apple-cheeked "country" quality about her complexion; the smooth, unmarked skin conjured up a vision of hot water and good soap.

"Will I like them?" she asked timidly.

"Why shouldn't you?"

"Will they like *me*?"

"We've a home to go back to," he growled.

Their names were Keith and Ada Parkinson.

3

The By-Pass

THE by-pass officially skirts the centre of Preston. Driving from the east up the hill, turn right instead of straight on to the town centre and that's it. Ninety-per-cent of traffic coming from the Pennines and making for Blackpool, Southport, Lytham St. Annes, Fleetwood, etc, turns onto this by-pass. The wise ten per-cent by-pass the by-pass, go straight ahead through Preston town centre and save both time and petrol.

The truth is—and despite its name—it is not a by-pass. The best that can be said is that it doesn't hit the bull; it dives straight through the "inner" and hits traffic lights every few hundred yards. It can (and often does) take longer to cross Preston on this so-called by-pass than it has taken to cross the rest of the county. It is not a motorway. Most of it is not even dual-carriageway. At holiday periods it can be the busiest and most frustrating stretch of road in the north of England.

Nor does this by-pass, which is not a by-pass, run through pleasant countryside. On the contrary, other than a stretch along one side which is a tatty municipal park-cum-playing fields, it is flanked by parades of shops, small and medium industrial sites, warehouses, public urinals (used by raging sufferers of countless traffic hold-ups) and garages—which, by the nature of things, are used even more frequently than the public urinals.

On the forecourt of one of the garages the mechanic, who was obviously no hit-it-with-a-hammer merchant, straightened up from a close examination of the Jag's engine and sighed before delivering his verdict.

"Main gasket's gone."

"Of all the bloody . . ." The driver compressed his lips, then grinned ruefully. "We've an appointment at Lytham at six."

"Not in this car. It's a fairly long job. The head has to come off for a start."

"Do you hire cars?"

"Sorry." The mechanic shook his head.

"A taxi?" There was a hint of desperation in the driver's tone.

The mechanic said, "It's as near twenty miles as makes no difference. It'll cost summat."

"Christ!"

"A taxi into town," suggested the mechanic. "Then there's a bus service or a train service to Blackpool. Then a bus from Blackpool to Lytham."

The driver didn't look enthusiastic.

"There is," said the mechanic, "a bus service between Blackburn and Blackpool. It passes here. It might be better. One change less."

"Often?" asked the driver.

"Not *that* often," admitted the mechanic. "Every two hours . . . I think."

"Can I use your telephone?" said the driver heavily.

"Sure. It's in the office."

But before the driver could leave the forecourt, his wife joined him from the short walk to a nearby shop to buy cigarettes. The driver moved his shoulders and spread his hands as he broke the news.

"We're buggered. The main gasket's blown."

"What do we do? Walk?"

She took the news with remarkable tranquillity. The double question was obviously not meant to be taken seriously, nevertheless . . .

"You'll have suitcases," observed the mechanic.

"Two beauts," said the driver sadly.

"Will you be leaving the car here for repair?"

"Where else?" The driver looked surprised at the question. "I've no intention of pushing the bloody thing home."

"Hang about a bit." The mechanic rubbed the nape of his neck. "I have a pal. About half a mile down the road. He has a van. *He* might run you in. I'll ask, if you like."

"A van?" The driver looked uncertain.

"Best I can do."

"But . . ." The driver waved his arms a little. "It's The Cave Hotel. We can't arrive there in a . . ."

"Ask your friend." The woman interrupted, and spoke to the mechanic. "Tell him we'd be very grateful. To Lytham Square, if he can. We'll take a taxi from there."

"I think he'll do it," smiled the mechanic.

He left the driver and his wife on the forecourt and hurried into the garage.

The woman was in her late fifties but looked younger, at least ten years younger. Her slim figure did justice to the dark tan trouser-suit and, in turn, the colour of the trouser-suit set off the lighter tan of a skin carefully and regularly subjected to sun-lamp treatment. Not that she tried to hide her age; merely that she'd looked after herself. She was hatless, and what had once been jet hair was liberally sprinkled with silver, but it was well-groomed and expertly cut. The impression was that she made decisions easily and without dither and that, more often than not, they were the right decisions.

The man was a few years her elder, but to a stranger meeting them for the first time, the age difference would not have been noticed. He could have been older or younger than her true age or her apparent age. He was completely bald and, as with so many bald men, a guess at his age would have been pure lucky-dip stuff. Despite his three-score-years-plus, he was a fit man. Squash and jogging squeezed the sweat from his pores and kept him trim. Physically, then, he was in good condition. Mentally he was a "worrier" and had two minor nervous breakdowns recorded in his medical history to prove the point. To quote his wife: "When there's nothing to worry about, he *still* worries. He worries *because* there's nothing to worry about. He's quite mad."

Their names were Ronald and Charlotte Powell.

4

Ron and Jim

"YOU should have phoned." Bathurst paused as the waiter bent to place the two double-whiskies and the jug filled with water and ice cubes on the table. He scrawled his initials on the proffered chitty before continuing, "I'd have sent the car out to pick you up."

"I had that in mind," lied Powell. "But Char seemed to fancy riding in a van."

They each added iced water to their whisky; Bathurst very little, Powell almost as much water as there was whisky. They were in a corner of the bar. Comfortable, and with enough privacy to talk knowing they would not be overheard. Bathurst brought a case from an inside pocket and offered cigars. Powell refused with a smile and a shake of the head.

"Still on the keep-fit lark?" Bathurst chose a cigar and returned the case to its pocket. He fished a cutter from his jacket pocket and snipped the end of the cigar clean. Then he took a lighter, placed the cigar between his lips, rolled the end in the flame and spoke between puffs. "Still play squash? Still jog every day?"

"We're over the hill, Jim." There was a touch of sadness in the remark and, having made it, Powell tasted his whisky.

"Balls." Bathurst leaned his head back and blew smoke towards the ceiling. "We're in our prime. I had a check-up a couple of months back. Not a thing wrong. Fit as a lop."

"Except for age. That's not an illness. That just happens."

"If I'm fit, *you're* fit," argued Bathurst.

"Sure, I'm fit. But twelve months older than last year. That's what I'm getting at. Most of it's behind us. I—y'know—keep remembering that."

"Keith doesn't think so. He's got himself a new woman."

"A new wife," corrected Powell.

"Same thing." Bathurst drank a third of the whisky-and-water in one swallow. "Some few years younger than he is, too, so I'm told."

"So I understand."

"He must think he's still a wick in his candle."

"Maybe." Powell allowed a smile to touch his lips. "I was sorry to hear about Hellen, though."

"Asthma." Bathurst drew on his cigar. "Hell of a thing, asthma. Remember? Four years back? Or is it five? I thought she was a goner then."

"It frightened me, too." For a moment Powell's eyes stared into the past. "A terrible thing to have to live with."

"For Keith too, I should think."

"Oh, yes. For Keith, too."

"Let's hope the new one hasn't some ailment or another."

"Eh? Oh—er—yes . . . quite."

There was a silence. Bathurst puffed contentedly at his cigar. Powell sipped his whisky-and-water and secretly wondered how much it might cost to have the Jag's gasket replaced.

Suddenly, as if silence was in some way offensive to him, Bathurst leaned forward, slapped his thigh with his free hand and said, "How goes it then Ron, old son? How's life treated you during the last year?"

"So-so," said Powell carefully. "No real set-backs. Nothing we couldn't handle."

"'We'," chuckled Bathurst. "Meaning you and Char. My Christ, Ron. Remember 'em? Char and Hellen in the old days? In the Mess?"

"Hellen hadn't asthma in those days," said Powell softly.

"What did we call 'em?" Bathurst chuckled at his memories. His shoulders shook gently and, to a keen ear, something not far from lasciviousness could be detected in the sound. "'The Iron Maidens'. By God, they were, too."

"Some of them were easy meat," murmured Powell awkwardly. "Char and Hellen weren't." He changed the subject and asked, "When's Keith due to arrive?"

"Should have been here an hour ago." The cigar travelled to and from Bathurst's lips. "He's a long trip. Held up somewhere maybe. I've put the meal back to nine o'clock. That should give him time."

There was another silence, then Powell took a longer-than-usual taste of his drink and blurted, "Why do we do it, Jim? This. Every year. What's the point?"

"Memories, old son," said Bathurst sombrely. "*Good* memories."

"Some of them aren't all that good."

"And, I owe." The tone was low and refused all argument. "It's a debt I can never repay." Then in a lighter tone, "Anyway, the girls like it. They look forward to catching up on things."

5

Emily and Char

EMILY BATHURST sat at the large, kidney-shaped dressing-table, touched her blue-rinsed hair lightly with a comb and spoke to Charlotte Powell via the dressing-table mirror. Charlotte was sitting on the edge of one of the twin beds. She was still wearing the tan-coloured trouser-suit and, as they talked, she smoked a cigarette, using the heavy glass ash-tray on the bedside table in which to tap the grey ash as it built up after each inhalation.

"Have you met Keith's new wife?" asked Emily.

"No. Have you?"

"No. Just that her name's . . . what is it?"

"Ada."

"Oh, yes. Ada." She touched her hair with the comb again. "I was very sorry to hear about Hellen. I—er—we didn't go to the funeral. Did you?"

"I went. Not Ron. He had important business commitments. But I went."

"Nice?"

"I've yet to see a nice funeral. It was adequate. She was dead, something had to be done with the body. Basically, that's all it boils down to." She drew on the cigarette and flipped a tiny scattering of ash into the tray. "That damned asthma thing. In one way it was a relief."

"Yes. I suppose so." The comb touched the hair again. "You were very close, weren't you? You and Hellen, I mean."

"Since the war years. We kept in touch. Not visiting. But we wrote to each other fairly regularly. Tittle-tattle. Gossip. But we kept in touch."

"It must have—er—hit you. More than it did the rest of us, I mean."

"I cried a little," admitted Charlotte. "Not much, but just a little. She'd had something of a raw deal. She hadn't deserved it."

"And this other woman—his new wife—she wasn't at the funeral?"

"She may have been. I wouldn't know.

Funerals . . . y'know. Half the people there you've never met before, or want to meet again."

Emily placed the comb carefully on the surface of the dressing-table then, in a quiet voice full of meaning, said, "He didn't waste much time."

"No." The single word seemed to be snapped off. Like biting into a stick of candy.

"It's going to be . . . difficult." Emily turned on the padded seat and faced Charlotte. "The men look forward to these annual get-togethers."

"God only knows why," sighed Charlotte. "They aren't what they were. None of them. Mine certainly isn't. A gasket blows, and it's panic stations. He wasn't always like that."

"They were once heroes, my dear." A whimsical smile accompanied the words. "They were looked upon as heroes. Recognised as such. And they *were*, and we *knew* they were. You, me, Hellen. We weren't fools, Charlotte. We recognised brave men."

"I suppose so," muttered Charlotte.

"I'll . . ." Emily looked mildly embarrassed. "May I have a cigarette, please?"

"I didn't know you smoked." Charlotte slipped a packet from her jacket pocket, opened it and offered the opened packet to the other woman.

"I don't. Very rarely." She picked one of the cigarettes from the packet. "So little that I rarely bother to buy any. But sometimes . . . Like now."

Emily held the tip of the cigarette in the flame of Charlotte's lighter, then inhaled awkwardly before she continued.

"Charlotte, over the years. Forty years, is it?"

"Forty years."

"We've come to know each other. Respect each other. You knew them before I did. You and Hellen, knew all three of them. As you know, I first met Jim in the hospital. Nursed him back to health, then married him. Since then . . . these annual re-unions. They're important. To them they're *very* important."

"Re-living past glories." There was impatience in the tone.

"Weren't they glorious?" asked Emily

solemnly. "At the time, didn't you think they were glorious?"

"I suppose so." There was reluctance in the admission. "It's just that . . . old men. That's what they are, even though they won't admit it."

"And equally old women," said Emily gently. "You're lucky. You've kept yourself looking younger than your age. Me? I don't fool myself. I'm an old broiler . . . and look it. Hellen, too. That asthma. It put years on her looks."

"And now he's landed some young tart." She squashed what was left of the cigarette into the ash-tray. "Don't ask me to be pleasant to her. He was in too much of a hurry."

"He was in a hurry." The quick smile was understanding. She raised and lowered the cigarette, before continuing, "Of course he was in a hurry. *He* knows how old he is, too."

"Don't ask me to be pleasant to her, that's all."

"Why not?" Her eyes held those of Charlotte. "It's Keith I'm thinking about, not his new wife. Nor his old wife, come to that. Keith and Ron and Jim. Ruin it for Keith, you'll ruin it for them all. Don't do that, my dear. Don't be as cruel as *that*."

Slowly, she rose from the edge of the bed. Slowly—almost, it seemed, carefully—she walked through the open door leading to the tiny lounge. As she walked, she placed her hands in the pockets of the trouser-suit. Again, slowly. Carefully. She stopped, facing the French window, and when she spoke it was in a measured, deliberate tone, as if voicing her thoughts—sharing her secrets with the sea beyond the green—but still easily audible to the woman sitting at the dressing-table.

"Emily, forgive me, but I've always looked upon you as an older woman. You're not, of course. We're of an age. Of the same generation. But you're wiser, or so I've always thought. Less worldly, perhaps, but wiser. Certainly kinder. More compassionate.

"I come to these ridiculous yearly junkets to see you. To re-charge my emotional batteries. To check that there's at least one nice person left in the world. A rotten world, Emily. You won't agree with that, I know, but oddly enough you're wise yet at the same time innocent. You can't see the rottenness. Can't or won't. But it's there. Lots of it. People aren't decent any more. Not like they used to be. Heroes? You spoke of heroes. There aren't any heroes left, Emily. They grew old. Mean. Weak. There aren't any left. Only memories of heroes, and each year those memories become more vague. Less certain. Less . . ."

She closed her mouth and stared out towards the sea for a moment, then continued in the same slow, deliberate tone.

"I have a sister. A sister a little like you. Maternal . . . if you know what I'm getting at. Not *quite* like you. She never married. Pity, that. This maternal quality. She'd have made some man a good wife. The right man, I mean. Not some bloody hero of today, who'll be a failure of tomorrow."

"Charlotte . . ."

"No! Leave me. Don't try to . . . y'know." She closed her mouth, compressed her lips, continued to stare through the French windows, then went on, "This sister. I wouldn't even tell *her* what I'm going to tell you. Shame, perhaps.

But with you I don't feel shame. You'll understand. Try to understand."

Another pause. Like an athlete gathering strength for a last effort.

"Ron and I. Remember Ron? What he used to be like? Remember? I'll tell you a secret, Emily darling. The only time we share the same bedroom is on these annual pilgrimages of remembrance. The same bedroom. Never, ever the same *bed*.

"Here we share the same room because we're ashamed of what we've become. We don't want people to know. Us! Char and Ron. No, we don't hate each other. I often wish we did. Hatred. There'd at least be the chance of a kiss-and-make-up ending to it. But, God, you can't kiss a—a piano. A chair. A table. That's what we are, pet. Part of the furniture. We 'go with the home', if you see what I mean. Over the years. Gradually. So gradually, we haven't even noticed. But it's five, six—maybe seven—years since we . . ." She swallowed and the first tear spilled and crawled slowly down her cheek. "That's a lousy thing to say. A lousy way to spoil *your* holiday. Why should you care? Why should anybody? Like you say, we're past it . . ."

"I didn't say that." Emily was at her shoulder, with a gentle, motherly arm around her waist.

"We're *all* past it. Except Keith. Him, too, but he won't accept it. Like me. He won't accept it. Just—y'know—don't expect me to be *pleasant* to her. To grin and simper at her, like an ageing barmpot. Not that, Emily. Not even for you."

6

Jim and Keith

JAMES BATHURST was still in the bar. To him a bar—any bar—was like a second home. His capacity for booze was quite something . . . Keith Parkinson remembered *that*, too. Even in the old days. Not women; he'd had no time for women, until he'd met up with Emily in the hospital. But tonsil varnish! My God, he could have drunk Rasputin under the table. In those days it had been beer, but recently—on the last few years of this re-union thing—it had turned to shorts. Whisky in the main, but if whisky wasn't immediately available, anything.

They were at the same table. Powell had left to shower and change for dinner. Bathurst was on his third double-whisky and, for what difference it had made, it might have been tap water. The cigar was half-smoked and he carefully rolled a grey cylinder of ash into the ash-tray. Parkinson was in the chair vacated by Powell and on the table before him was a half-pint glass of cider.

"I'm sorry we're so late," he said for the third time.

"No sweat, old son." Bathurst moved the cigar, before raising it to his lips. "It's a hell of a pull from East Anglia. My fault. I should have realised."

"The bloody motorways . . ."

"No sweat," repeated Bathurst. "I've re-timed the meal. Not to worry."

"I asked the porter. He said you were in here."

"Where else?" grinned Bathurst.

"Ada's gone up with the luggage and to titivate herself up a bit."

"Ah!" Bathurst (*for* Bathurst) looked slightly embarrassed, and said, "I don't have to tell you. About Hellen. How sorry we were. You—er—you got the wreath?"

"Yes. Thanks." Parkinson tasted the cider. He changed the subject. "The others here? Ron and Char? Emily, of course?"

"All present and correct," said Bathurst solemnly.

"Forty years," mused Parkinson.

"Forty years," agreed Bathurst. "Let's

make it a dinger, Keith. We might not all be here for the fiftieth . . ." He stopped, blew out his cheeks in self-disgust and shook his head. "Trust me! I didn't mean to trample on corns, old son. Sorry."

"Jim." Parkinson tasted the cider, returned the glass to the table, then wiped non-existent moisture from his lips with the fingers of one hand. "Jim, there's something needs saying. Passing around . . . if you'll do it. I can't."

"Sure, but . . ."

"I almost didn't come this year."

"That's understandable. I mean with Hellen . . ."

"That's why." Parkinson's voice carried soft, but savage, urgency. "Hellen isn't here this year. *Nor is her ghost*. She'd want it that way. You knew her. You knew her when she was . . . before that damned asthma changed her. *That* was Hellen. The *real* Hellen. She'd want this to be a celebration. Not a wake. You see what I'm getting at?"

"I'll let the others know," promised Bathurst. "On the quiet."

"And not to feel awkward. See? Talk about her. I don't mind. Ada won't mind.

I can talk about her. We both can. It's—y'know—not a forbidden subject. Act naturally. Y'know, like always. Otherwise I'll wish we *hadn't* come."

"Heard and understood, lad." Bathurst nodded ponderously. "Leave it to me. I'll see it gets around."

7

Ada

SHE was out of her depth—well out of her depth—and knew it. This place, this Cave Hotel, it was a completely new experience and at the moment it frightened her. When she'd made to carry one of the suitcases, the porter had looked almost offended. No, not really offended. A little bit contemptuous. "Excuse me, ma'am. That's what *I'm* here for." Polite enough. Nobody could fault his manners. But the *way* he'd said it. The subtle, hidden meaning. And when they'd left the lift and they'd reached the room —the *rooms*—and he'd opened the door. "After you, madam." Then, "This is the bathroom, madam. This is the private lounge, madam. The French windows lead out to your balcony." And finally, "Is that all, madam?" and the pause at the open door before he left.

She'd stammered, "My—my husband.

He's—er—he's in the bar. With Mr. Bathurst. If you'll—er—y'know—see *him* . . ." and then she'd dried up, flush-faced and embarrassed, and the porter had bobbed his head and gone, closing the door silently but firmly behind him.

A tip? She supposed he'd expected a tip, but she wasn't sure. *Did* you tip at these places? And if you did, when? As things were done for you or at the end just before you left? And how big a tip? That porter? A pound? He'd have expected at least a pound . . . and just for carrying a couple of suitcases from the lift and opening a couple of doors. That was outrageous! But that's what he'd have *expected*.

And because she *hadn't* tipped him—because she hadn't been sure—he'd made her feel uncomfortable. Out of place. Good heavens, she might not be on a par with the usual run of folk who could afford to stay at The Cave Hotel, but she was as good as any silly hotel porter. She hadn't had to feel inferior to *him*.

She unpacked the suitcases and carefully stowed the clothes away in the wardrobes and drawers . . . and wished she'd never come.

Even Keith. He'd left her alone in this strange, alien world while he'd gone in search of his friend. It wasn't fair. He must have *known*. Somebody born and brought up in the wilds of Suffolk; who'd lived on a farm all her life; who'd looked after her widowed mother until the mother had died and then . . . Dammit, it wasn't *fair*! These sort of places. You saw them on the telly, in films and plays, but everybody knew exactly what to do, exactly what to wear, exactly what to say. But the little things—the important things—the things that mattered and made the difference between you being a fool or not . . . they never showed you *them*.

And the others? Bathurst and his wife? Powell and his wife? If a place like this was what they were used to, how on earth could *she* fit in? There was a dinner. Then tomorrow there was this annual party thing. And, all right, Keith knew them. He'd known them a long time. So had Hellen. They'd both known them, but *she* only knew them by name. By the stories told by both Keith and Hellen.

Six of them. There'd always been six. How long? Forty years. And now there was only five, because she could never *ever* be a real part. The odd one out. The country bumpkin. What else, in a place like this and with Keith and his friends of such long standing?

Oh God! She wished she hadn't come.

8

Jim and Emily

"HAVE you seen her yet?"

Bathurst bawled the question through the open bathroom door and above the steady hiss of the shower. He sudded his thick-limbed body with expensive toilet soap, aided by a sponge not much smaller than a football. He used unnecessary vigour; twisting and wrestling his arms and legs as if physically fighting the needle-spray. The heat, generated by the near-scalding water and his own exertions turned his skin deep pink and made the ugly, misshapen scar across his lower abdomen stand out white and vivid.

His wife didn't answer. She might even not have heard him. She'd changed into an evening dress; a simple, russet-coloured affair whose very simplicity, combined with its immaculate "cut' and "fall' gave evidence of its cost. She was standing at the full-length mirror let into the wardrobe door, arranging the single string of pearls around her neck.

Bathurst turned off the tap, shook his head much as a dog shakes moisture from its hair, stepped onto the cork matting and reached for one of the king-sized towels waiting on the heated rail.

"I was saying," he repeated, "Have you seen her yet?"

"Who?" His wife played the feminine game of deliberately not understanding.

"Keith's new missus."

"No. Why should I?" She gave the pearls a tiny pat of satisfaction.

"It's just that . . ." He sawed the towel across his back and shoulder-blades. Rubbed his hair, as he said, "Y'know, knowing you. I thought you might have gone along. To welcome her, like."

"I'm not nosey." She chose to sound slightly offended.

"Not *nosey*." He started on his trunk-like legs. "I'm not saying that. Just—y'know—to make her welcome."

"Surely, you saw her first."

"No." The towel worked away at his front and arms. "Keith left her to find her own way to their rooms while he sorted me out in the bar."

"He hasn't much thought," she observed drily.

"No. He wanted me to pass the word round, see?"

"What word?"

"About Hellen. He doesn't mind if we talk about her. That sort of thing." He tossed the towel onto the cork-bottomed chair and walked naked into the bedroom. "Not to feel embarrassed."

"We won't be embarrassed talking about Hellen," she said gently. "On the other hand, we *might* be embarrassed talking to the woman who's taken Hellen's place."

"Hey!" He stared. "That's not like you."

"I wouldn't know. It's a situation I've never met before."

"Dammit, give her a chance. Remember who she is. She's *Keith's* wife."

"Oddly enough, that's why we might be embarrassed."

She watched him as he sorted through the clean underclothes laid out on the bed. As he struggled into the string vest and short underpants. As he sat on the edge of the bed to pull on his socks.

She said, "I think Char hates her already."

"Char? Has she met her, then?"

"No, but she thought a lot about Hellen."

"Char's a silly cow," he pronounced bluntly. "She was a bit that way when we first knew her. She's got worse as she's grown older."

"She and Ron sleep in different rooms."

"Eh?"

"It's a marriage in name only."

"That's a bloody fine thing!"

"One reason why she already hates Keith's new wife. That's *my* reading of things."

"You women . . ." He stood up from the bed and reached for his trousers. "Two of you together, and that's all you can talk about."

"Men don't, of course?"

"I'm not saying we don't. We just don't make out we don't."

"Her own marriage. And Hellen can't have been much of a mate, what with the asthma."

"We're getting on in years, lass." He hoisted the braces over his shoulders, suddenly realised he hadn't yet put on his shirt, and growled, "Damn!" He unyanked the braces and reached for the shirt. "See what I mean? Old age and bloody stupidity."

"That's what Char's frightened of," she said slowly.

"What?"

"Growing old."

"She say that?"

"Not in as many words. But I think that's what it boils down to."

"How daft can you get?" He wrestled his way into the shirt. "We're all getting older, and at the same speed. Good God, you can't stop it. You can't slow it down. Being frightened's barmy. It's like being frightened of a thunderstorm. There's damn-all you can do about it. Just sit back and enjoy it."

He sat down on the bed again. Held out an arm at a time and allowed her to fix the cuff-links. It was done without asking. They both knew each other well enough. His thick fingers couldn't easily cope and there'd have been a rising temper and bad language.

In a strangely gentle tone he said, "We've been lucky, old girl. No problems with that part of our marriage."

"We've been lucky," she agreed.

"And does she say it's Ron's fault?"

"There's a suggestion. Rather more than a suggestion."

"Has he a bit on the side? Is that it?"

"No." She shook her head very positively. "She'd have said. It's not that."

"What's she want, then? Some young ram? Ron's like the rest of us, y'know. He's getting a bit past it."

She stepped back to allow him to stand up, unzip, tuck the shirt into his waistband and zip up again. Once more, he pulled the braces over his shoulders.

Very gently, very solemnly, she said, "I don't think they love each other any more."

"Oh, my Christ!"

"She's worked to keep herself looking younger than her age."

"She wants to have a word with—what's-her-name—Barbara Cartland. Feed him a jar of honey a day. See if that does the trick."

"It's serious, Jim."

"It's none of our business."

"Oh, yes." The concerned expression got through to him. "She's our friend. One of our oldest friends. So is Ron. So is Keith. These annual get-togethers. They mean a great deal . . ."

"They're bloody important."

"Especially to you three men. If Char gets the bit between her teeth, she could ruin everything."

His nostrils quivered and he growled, "If Char says as much as one word out of place, she'll feel her bloody age all right. She'll think she's still a bloody school-kid, and that I'm the headmaster giving her the dressing-down to end all dressing-downs."

9

Char and Ron

"AREN'T you ready, yet?"

Charlotte Powell did nothing to hide her impatience. Dressed and ready, she watched her husband struggle to place the knot in order that the white rose emblem sat in a neat position on the dark blue tie. She was an attractive woman; for her age, an extremely attractive woman. And part of her attractiveness was due to the care with which she chose her clothes. She knew, for instance, that trouser-suits set off her boyish figure far better than any outfit which included a skirt, therefore she always wore slacks or moderately expensive trouser-suits. Even her night attire was pyjama trousers and matching jacket which didn't hang shapelessly from her slim body. Her hair, too; no colouring, no unnecessary frivolity, but instead a simple cut and shape (which, in fact, was not *so* simple) which in some mystical way suggested a "mannish" look, but at the same time added to her overall femininity.

Her present suit was of black, artificial silk with thin white piping at the edge of the collar and on the flaps of the pockets. A tiny frill of a high-necked, white blouse made tasteful contrast at the V of the jacket and set off the tan of her face. The shoes were of black patent leather, with inch-high heels; comfortable, no-nonsense shoes which matched the rest of the outfit to perfection. Her only jewellery was her wedding band, a wrist-watch and a blue-black oval brooch with a round, scooped-out centre lined with tiny diamonds, which was pinned to the lapel of the jacket.

Care and taste had gone into the choice of clothes, and the result couldn't be faulted.

Ron, on the other hand, wore standard grey flannel trousers, a white shirt and a dark blue blazer. The expression "fits where it touches" sprang to mind and was emphasised by his slightly stooped shoulders and his polished bald head.

Together they typified a marriage gone sour. Two sons, one happily married with a well-loved child of his own, the other scrambling his way through law courts with dreams of one day becoming an eminent QC, kept their marriage from complete and open destruction, but only just. And yet . . .

They were the same Ron and Char whose early years had been filled with laughter; who'd worked together, played together, taken their then life by the scruff of the neck and had had no doubts that they'd win a way through to the top of the heap. Such dreams. Such plans. Such ambitions. And almost as a natural by-product, such loving. Always walking hand-in-hand. The sudden kiss as a bore of mutual affection demanded outward manifestation. And the physical love-making; day or night, any hour of the twenty-four; indoors or out; in bed, of course, but also under the shower or in a shared bath; sometimes, when they were driving, in the semi-privacy of a lay-by; out walking, in the shelter of some bluebell wood, hidden among the sweet-smelling secrecy of a corn field, in the secluded slopes of sand dunes. Anywhere. Everywhere. Not merely man and wife. Char and Ron, lovers whose wild passion promised to last forever.

Forever!

"Stop fiddling with that stupid tie."

"I like it right." His voice was without expression. "If it isn't right, it *does* look stupid."

"I want to be there—settled—before Keith and his woman arrive."

"His *wife*," he corrected mildly.

"I want to see how *she* makes the grand entrance."

He touched the knot for a last time, turned, sighed, then remarked, very softly, "You really are a bit of a bitch, aren't you?"

10

Keith and Ada

"THEY won't like me."

The remark was made in a tremulous, little-girl-lost voice, and the truth was, she wasn't too far from tears.

"They'll like you." Keith Parkinson's tone was both soothing and firm. He knew (or thought he knew) how his new wife was feeling; knew (or thought he knew) how he'd have been feeling in her position. He also truly believed it to be a form of "stage fright" and that, once they'd reached the dining room, the others would go out of their way to put her at her ease. He said, "They'll like you, because they like me and *you're* my wife. It's that simple."

"No. They'll compare me with Hellen."

"Now, why on earth . . ."

"They may not do it deliberately. Not openly. But they *will*."

"And if they do?" he conceded.

"I'm—I'm not at all like Hellen."

"Of course you're not. Have I ever suggested you should be?"

"I'm a lot younger. Younger than any of you."

"You're no teenager, pet." The words were said kindly and carried no hint of criticism. "They can't accuse me of *that*."

"They won't accuse *you* of anything. It's *me* they'll blame."

"Blame?" He looked puzzled.

"You know what I mean."

"No." He stepped closer to her and took her hands in his. "You're my wife, Ada. You're not my fancy woman. You're not my mistress. You're my *wife*. You're not like Hellen, because I wouldn't have married anybody remotely like Hellen. I didn't marry you to *remind* me. I married you because, without Hellen, I was lost. Lonely. Unable to cope. I also married you because I loved you. Still love you. All right, you're a few years younger than I am. A few years younger than any of us are. Why should that matter? You're a mature woman—a very kind and understanding woman—and I'm damned if I can see the logic of the suggestion that I should have hunted around, looking for some sex-starved biddy of my own age, just to keep the books nicely balanced. I married you for the best reason in the world. The only reason that matters. I was lonely. I was a broken man. Hellen—God rest her soul—couldn't help having that infernal disease, but it damn near killed both of us. She knew what was happening. More important, *she loved you, too*."

"I—I like to think so."

"Don't ever doubt it, pet," he said gently. "I don't have to remind you. She wasn't too keen, at first, when I suggested a live-in-house-help-cum-companion, but what else? I was away for days at a time. I didn't know what the devil was happening at home. How she was coping. Whether or not she could fight her way through every attack without me being there. Without *somebody* being there to help. That much we both owe you. That much can never be repaid." He paused, smiled, then continued, "And we've both a clear conscience . . . don't forget that. Although we lived under the same roof, we didn't romp in the hay because I had a sick wife."

"We didn't 'romp in the hay', as you put

it, until after we were married." Her tone carried mild censure.

"I know." The gentle solemnity returned to his voice. "*And* you were a virgin. It came as quite a shock. A very pleasant surprise." The smile came back and broadened into a grin. "That's a claim Hellen couldn't have made. Nor, at a guess, can either Char or Emily. You have 'em, pet. Don't let them knock you. You're the only *good* person amongst us."

"I love you," she said simply.

He leaned forward and kissed her lightly on the forehead, then said, "Me you, too, but let's keep Chinamen out of this."

11

Skirmish

THEY met at the lift. Ron and Char and Keith and Ada. The timing, although not planned, was immaculate. Both Ron and Keith reached for the button at the same time. Ron pulled back his hand and Keith it was who thumbed the red disc which illuminated the "Lift Coming" sign.

As they waited those few moments Keith and Ron indulged in a double-grip handshake.

"God, you don't look a day older."

"You look as fit as ever, too."

"It must be the grub Char feeds you." Then, turning to the waiting Ada, "Darling, meet two very nice people. Char and Ron. Char, Ron . . . meet Ada."

Ron shook hands and grinned genuine pleasure.

Char kept her arms by her side, eyed the younger woman from top to toe, then drawled, "So, you're Keith's new wom . . ."

"You're Keith's new wife." Ron interrupted the forbidden word. His voice was a shade louder than it need have been. "The new member of the crew. Welcome aboard."

The lift doors whispered open. Ron placed a firm hand on his wife's back, ushered her into the tiny cubicle, then followed. Then Ada. Then Keith. Ron pressed the "Ground Floor" button and the doors sighed themselves together.

"Hellen was my oldest friend," said Char flatly.

"She was my friend, too," countered the younger woman.

The two men exchanged worried glances.

Char said, "We met during the war years. We were friends—close friends—till the day she died."

"Yes. She talked about you, a lot."

Keith looked at his wife. Quietly, without being offensive, this younger woman was holding her own. Char, he knew, had a waspish tongue when the spirit moved her, but this younger, Suffolk woman who'd taken Hellen's place had suddenly found steel. She was a different person to the frightened wife he'd had to comfort in the privacy of their bedroom.

"We'll miss her," said Char.

"Of course." The smile was sweet, and quite false. "We'll *all* miss her. Keith especially."

"Now he has you, of course . . ."

"I'm not Hellen," interrupted Ada.

"I wasn't suggesting you . . ."

"I was with her, up to less than an hour before her death. Frankly, I wouldn't *want* to be Hellen. I wouldn't want to suffer like she suffered."

The older woman compressed her lips.

Ada continued, "I nursed her for months before the end. I cleaned her, then laid her out. I wept while I was doing it, but we were close friends and our friendship demanded that no stranger be allowed that sort of intimacy." The pause was beautifully timed, then she ended, "I think I saw you at the funeral . . . with all the wreaths and flowers."

"Are you suggesting . . . ."

"I'm suggesting nothing, Mrs. Powell." Again, the smile of quiet victory. "As I recall, you brought the topic up. Hellen

. . . and what good friends you were. Just that she had other friends. Not as long-standing, but every bit as close."

The lift slowed to a halt, the doors slid open.

Ron said, "Right. Let's find where the dining room is."

12

The Meal

THE green-and-gold dining room was almost full. A handful of early diners had already left—their tables cleared and re-set with pristine and geometric precision, ready for the next morning's breakfast—but, apart from these departures, every table was occupied. Waiters and waitresses, in outfits matching the dark green of the carpet, scurried between the tables, watched by the head waiter resplendent in full evening dress complete with white carnation. At many tables cigars and cigarettes were being smoked, but half-a-dozen, silent-running fans carefully let high into the "Old Gold" hessian-covered wall panels killed any hint of stale tobacco smoke; as each ash-tray was used—before its glass base was even covered with ash or spent cigarettes—it was whisked away and replaced by a sparklingly clean mate.

This was The Cave Hotel. You paid for

it, but if you were prepared to pay for it, you *got* it.

They sat at an oval table; three opposite three, but with an intimacy an oblong table would have denied. When the four had arrived from the lift, Jim and Emily had stood up from their chairs. Emily had allowed Keith, then Ron to kiss her cheek.

Keith had said, "Emily, Jim . . . this is Ada."

Emily had stepped closer, held the younger woman gently by the upper arms, touched cheeks and whispered, "Don't be scared, my dear. Relax and enjoy yourself."

A little awkwardly, Jim had extended an arm and, as they shook hands, had grinned broadly and murmured, "I approve. I *definitely* approve."

In a very soft voice Char had said, "You never *did* have taste," but only Ron had heard her, and he made believe he hadn't.

Then there had been the banter. Jim, of course, had been the leader, but Keith and Ron had joined in. So had Emily and, to a lesser degree, Char; Char, it seemed, had been prepared to content herself with ignoring Ada's existence for the time being. Ada, on her part, had had the sense to realise that, while not being deliberately ignored by the others, this opening play of the get-together had not been able to include her because it had been based on memories of which she had no knowledge. She had, therefore, sat and smiled at jokes she hadn't understood; happy to allow the others freedom to warm themselves up prior to enjoyment of the meal.

The wine waiter had produced the wine list, and Jim had made great play of studying the four pages of choice.

"Red for meat, white for fowl or fish," he'd muttered.

"Oh, my God! If that's the limit of his knowledge, make it Red Biddy, all round."

"Wouldn't go with duck, old son."

"Who's having duck?"

Emily had said, "I think I might have duck."

"A duck for a duck, eh?"

"For a dear old duck."

"Now, don't be cheeky Keith. I can run *you* the length of the promenade and not be breathless."

"Y'know, I might just hold you to that."

"Anyway, old son." Jim had turned to

the wine waiter. "Which do you suggest? Red and white."

The wine waiter had offered his advice.

"Fair enough. Three of each. If anybody's mad enough to prefer rosé, we'll mix 'em."

The wine waiter had left and Jim had said, "For starters, prawn cocktails. I've already ordered. That's one thing we all like."

"Ada?" Emily had looked questioningly at Keith's wife.

"Oh, that's fine. Lovely."

Then more banter. More laughter. The wine waiter had returned to perform the ritual of allowing Jim to taste the ordered wine.

"Talk about pearls before swine."

"You're supposed to smell it, Jim. Smell it, before you taste it."

The wine waiter had allowed himself a tight, slightly disapproving, smile.

"That's fine, old son." Jim had nodded, happily. "Ignore these rabble-rousing erks. Three of each . . . and thanks for your help."

"Oh, and—er—coffee. We'd like it here at the table. Not in the sun lounge."

"I'll arrange it, sir."

"And tell 'em to have the liqueurs handy."

"Yes, sir."

The wine waiter had left and almost immediately a waiter and a waitress had arrived with the prawn cocktails; tall glasses filled to within a quarter-of-an-inch of the brim with shredded salad, baby prawns and the dressing unique to The Cave. The rim of each glass was hidden beneath a ring of great, king prawns and the truth was that Ada had stared at this expensive concoction and hadn't been too sure how to begin. The array of cutlery was a little overpowering and the old rule of "start at the outside and work in" didn't seem to apply. The men were still busy chatting to each other and Char made no move; she watched Ada and seemed to be willing her to make a fool of herself.

Emily, too, saw the mild dismay in Ada's expression and the cold contemptuous gaze of Char.

Emily sighed and, apparently talking to herself, said, "This is ridiculous. However, fingers were made before forks."

She lifted one of the king prawns from

its resting place and began to nibble at it. Ada gave a tiny smile of thanks and followed suit. Char breathed deeply then she too—and the men—used their fingers to find a way of getting the long spoons into the main body of the prawn cocktails.

It was quite a meal. Emily had roast duckling with orange. Char, too, had roast duckling, but with black cherries. Ada had blue trout, with melted butter. The men had meat dishes. Jim, steak voronov and Keith and Ron gammon with pineapple. For desserts it was crêpe suzette and banana flambée for the women and ice cream with liqueur all round for the men.

It was, indeed, quite a meal and, until the coffee, the Tia Maria, the Drambuie and the Cognac arrived there was little talk other than appreciative remarks about the fine food.

But with the arrival of the coffee, and the lighting of cigars and cigarettes, the small-talk and the not-so-small-talk gathered momentum. The wine had all gone; the women had had their share, but most of it had been downed by the men . . . red and white. And now, the liqueurs loosened their tongues even more. It was past eleven o'clock, and the dining room was more than half empty of customers.

Afterwards—long afterwards—Emily tried to remember how it had started. What had led up to it. How a silly conversation had opened the way for Char's outrageous remark.

Fleetwood had come into it. Fleetwood, and a possible trip to Fleetwood by Keith and Ada the following day. And kippers. Fleetwood kippers, and who was going to have Fleetwood kippers for breakfast next morning. The merits of and difference between various local kippers. Fleetwood kippers, Whitby kippers, Scottish kippers, kippers caught and smoked along the south coast. Somehow, the drink had made kippers a subject worthy of long and erudite conversation and, because he travelled a lot, Keith was elevated to the position of expert. Which kippers did he prefer? Which, in his considered opinion, were the kippers most expertly smoked? Which were the fattest and tastiest? And, for a few moments, Keith had held centre-stage. And (the truth) he enjoyed it. With slightly-drunken solemnity he pronounced opinions and reasons for those opinions.

And from kippers to fish generally and shellfish in particular. Mussels, cockles, whelks, winkles. And, of course, oysters.

Jim said, "Tell you what *I'm* gonna do, tomorrow. Into Blackpool, see? And half-a-dozen of those fresh blue points. Straight from the open stall on the front. Vinegar—lots of vinegar—a touch of pepper, and straight from the shell. Down, without even touching the sides."

Then there was a pause. A small silence; as if each of them was getting a second wind, prior to winding on to discuss some other equally unimportant topic.

And very plainly—very deliberately—Char shattered that silence.

"Keith, I'm surprised *you* didn't have oysters this evening. Oysters—lots of oysters—garnished with powdered rhino horn. And champagne, too. They tell me champagne helps a lot. You're likely to need help, aren't you? All the help you can get. After all, you're going to bed with a tart young enough to be your daughter."

And the silence changed. From warm, boozey silence into an angry, livid silence in which the weight of loathing could not, for the moment, find expression. Thunder gathered in Jim's expression. Ada blushed to an embarrassed scarlet and lowered her head until she was staring at the napkin crumpled in front of her on the table. Keith's eyes blazed from a face white with sudden fury. He made to stand up, but Ron beat him to it.

Ron, too, was red with a mix of anger and embarrassment. He rose with a suddenness which sent his chair tippling backwards onto the carpet, and the other diners in the room turned and stared. His whole face—even his bald head—was scarlet with humiliation and outrage; scarlet and with the sheen of sweat. For a moment, he stood, head lowered and steadying himself with his clenched fists resting on the surface of the table. Then he raised his head and, when he spoke, his voice was hoarse but steady.

"Ladies and gentlemen—Keith—Ada—and you, too, Emily and Jim. Because this foul-minded creature happens to be my wife, I owe you all an apology. A very deep, very humble apology. I am her husband. At this moment, I'm ashamed to have to make that admission, but I *am* her husband, she carries my name—even though she shames it with monotonous regularity—therefore, because *she* hasn't the good manners to apologise, I must do it for her. Please forgive us the unforgiveable. Jim, if you want us to leave we'll leave tonight—now."

"Don't be so damned stupid. Of course you're staying. A dirty-minded old cow isn't going to be allowed to spoil *our* party."

Ron muttered, "Thank you." Then he continued, "Keith, you know these aren't empty words. They aren't easy to say."

"Forget it, mate. *You* haven't spoiled your manners."

"And you, Ada. We aren't *all* like this wife of mine. She's rather unique. A mutation, perhaps. I'm truly sorry to have imposed her upon you. Perhaps I should have come here alone, knowing the sort of person she is." He paused to moisten his lips. "Keith—Ada—it's a little late, and it's probably completely out of place in the circumstances but I, for one, wish you every happiness in your marriage."

Emily murmured, "I'll second that."

"Hellen. We all knew Hellen. We all loved Hellen. Had it been possible, we'd have wanted Hellen here with us today. Tomorrow. But she's dead, and that's a thing we can't alter. Instead, we have you, Ada, and Keith's been very lucky . . . twice. I only wish *I* could have been as lucky *once*."

He turned, picked up the chair and sat down. He met nobody's eyes. He'd said what he'd wanted to say. Perhaps he'd said too much. If so, he didn't give a damn.

Char picked her handbag up from the carpet alongside her chair. She stood up and, straight-backed, walked from the dining room. Her face was set and expressionless.

Nobody spoke until Char was beyond the door, then Jim cleared his throat, noisily, and said, "Right. Who wants more coffee? More liqueur?"

Ada raised her head and, in a soft voice, said, "Keith, have you the keys to the car?"

"Yes. Why?"

"I'd like some air. My coat's in the back, and my headscarf's in the glove compartment."

"Look, it's late. It's not wise . . ."

"I won't go far. I'll stay within sight of the hotel."

"Shall I go with you?"

"No. Alone, please."

Keith looked worried, nevertheless he fished the car keys from the pocket of his trousers and handed them across the table.

13

The Promenade

LYTHAM ST. ANNES' promenade is a strangely private and friendly place. Even at midnight, with no other person in sight, it feels "safe". The lights on the road beyond the green give illumination enough and, on the promenade itself, there are older-fashioned lamps whose glow is a little less brilliant. This double street-lighting, plus the lights from the major hotels, demolishes all shadows in which trouble might be lurking.

And yet, it is not a gaudy place. The broad belt of grass softens the overall effect and the cheerful, noisy, all-night brashness of Blackpool has not yet stretched far beyond Squires Gate. The objectionable drunks rarely stagger farther south than Fairhaven, and not often that far. It is as if a barrier has been erected—a line drawn on a map and an ordinance passed which says, "Thus far, but no farther. The

Blackpool hell-raising, innocent or otherwise, stops here. Beyond this point there is tranquillity and peace". And some distance south of that cut-off point you will find Lytham St. Annes and its delightful promenade.

The breeze from the sea flapped her head-scarf and carried the tang of salt-water to her nostrils. She had (she thought) drunk a little too much. Far more than normal. Not that she was drunk, or even mentally befuddled in any way. Just that she wasn't a drinker, and the wine *had* flowed.

She walked slowly and allowed her thoughts freedom to wander along paths of their own choice. Hellen, for example. Dear, patient Hellen. Their relationship had been unique; after a shaky start, they'd laughed at the same jokes a few times and, thereafter, they'd grown to love each other. Childless, Hellen had (perhaps) looked upon her as an *ex-officio* daughter. Perhaps. But that had only been part of it. A small part. She'd also been nurse and friend. *Ex-officio* younger sister, even. All these things, and more.

Because Hellen *had* been Hellen, and the others (Jim, Emily, Ron, Char—yes, even

Char—and especially Keith) had lost something precious beyond price when she'd died. Come to that so had *she*, but it was understandable that the others might forget that.

She wished . . .

Well, what *did* she wish?

Basically, she wished they'd not come to this annual all-pals-together thing, but that was real fairy-tale stuff. Even Hellen never missed. *Had* never missed. (God, it was so easy to think she was still alive!) Almost every day, she'd talked about it. Reminisced. Re-lived all the other years, and the way-out things they'd got up to. All about Jim, and Ron, and Char, and Emily. She'd really loved them. Last year, in fact, she'd suggested they make it *seven*—take her (Ada) along to share the high jinks—but, in the nicest possible way, Keith had scotched the idea. Six was the number—the original six—and six it must remain.

Until this year . . .

Still six, of course. But not the *original* six. That was the mistake they'd made; the mistake she wished they *hadn't* made.

She wished . . .

She wished Char had been a bit more

charitable. A bit less bitter. She (Ada) had never expected to be "admitted", if that was the right word. She hadn't expected *that*. Forty years (as she understood it, this thing had been going on for almost half a century) and after that length of time you don't admit newcomers. Especially newcomers who only have a vague idea of what it's all about. If anybody was to blame, it was Keith. He'd been too *sure*. He shouldn't have been. He should have had more sense. He should either have come alone, or have been content with letting her sit on the sideline. Watch, perhaps. Enjoy seeing *him* enjoying himself.

Instead of which . . .

No. She couldn't *really* blame Char. All this "best friend" business. A thing she (Ada) could never properly understand. All her life she'd been too busy for best friends. A sick mother and a demanding brother. And yet . . . maybe Hellen had been *her* best friend too. A very dear friend. At the very least *that*. Somebody the like of which she'd never met before. Somebody who knew how to love and who, in return, was loved. Alive. Despite her sickness, so very much alive. And cheerful. And kind . . .

And oh how she wished somebody had *laughed* at that oysters-and-champagne remark. That's all it had needed. All right, it hadn't been *meant* as a joke. It had been a snide and nasty jibe. But if it had been *taken* as a joke. A bit bawdy, perhaps. A bit beyond the limit of good manners. But, good heavens, she wasn't some simpering teenager. She, too, could have laughed. She could have accepted it—*would* have accepted it—as drink getting the better of politeness. That was how it *should* have been treated. Instead of which . . .

All this hail-fellow-well-met stuff and, underneath the surface, such touchiness. As if—silly as it sounded—the death of one had reminded the others of their own mortality. God, they *were* getting old. They *were* past their best years. But so what? The same age as Hellen but, despite the asthma, she'd accepted . . .

"Ada, may I talk with you, please?"

"What!"

The voice startled her. Ron's voice, but she'd thought she was alone on the promenade. She hadn't seen him hurry up behind her. Hadn't heard him. Not surprising, really. She'd been deep in thought. Mentally miles away in an orgy of wishful thinking.

He said, "I'm sorry if I . . ."

"No. It's all right. It's just that—y'know —I didn't hear you. Didn't see you."

"May I talk to you?" he repeated, and his voice was apologetic. Gentle, and a little weary.

"Of course."

The truth was, she didn't want to. Didn't want to talk to anybody. Just to walk; to breathe the sea air and sort things out a little.

There was a bench, facing out to sea. He motioned towards it with one of his hands.

"May we?"

She shrugged.

"I'm . . ." The quick smile was sorrowful. "Y'see, I've had more to drink than usual." Then hurriedly, "Not that I'm drunk. Not that I don't know what I'm saying. Just that . . ."

"Why not?"

She walked to the bench. Briskly. She sat down and stared out to sea. Out there in the darkness—not far from the horizon

—a tiny red light twinkled. Some boat. Sailing south, obviously. Red light to port, therefore it was sailing south. That or anchored. It wasn't moving—didn't *seem* to be moving . . . maybe the distance gave the impression of not moving. It was certainly *facing* south.

He sat down alongside her. Near, but not touching. He, too, stared out to sea. He linked his fingers and gripped them between his thighs. As if his bladder was full, but he was unable to relieve himself. He sat there, in that miserable posture, for all of a minute before he spoke.

He mumbled, "It's—it's about Char . . ."

"I wish you wouldn't," she said gently.

"The—the things she comes out with sometimes."

"It's not important."

"It *is* important. It's important to *me*."

"Ah!"

"I mean . . . to call you a tart. That's not . . ."

"How do you know I'm not?" she asked brusquely.

"Eh?"

"Oh, never mind." Her voice was tempered with impatience. She hoisted the collar of her coat a little higher, and continued to watch the red light out at sea. In a calmer tone, she said, "That apology was a little silly. And quite unnecessary."

"You—you mean you . . ."

"It made you sound pompous."

"Oh!"

"Perhaps you *are* pompous." She saw no reason to play nursemaid to a man older than herself. "Perhaps that's why your wife *said* those things."

"I—I don't . . ."

"To goad you into making a fool of yourself."

"Did I . . ." The whispered question wasn't completed.

"I don't know you." Her tone was uncompromising. "I know you as 'Ron'. Beyond that, nothing. What Keith's told me. What Hellen told me. But *I* don't know you. That you're Char's husband, and that you're frightened to death of her. That's all *I* . . ."

"I'm not frightened of her. What makes you think . . ."

"Oh, come on!"

"She's a very—very dominating woman. She likes to get her own . . ."

"And you're as weak as water." She was suddenly very irritated by this whining creature alongside her. "She likes to get her own way. So what? *All* women like to have their own way. It's part of their nature. And they'll have their own way if they aren't stopped. Then what happens? Unless they grab themselves—see the error of their own ways—they want, and want, and want. Eventually, they don't even know what they *do* want. They've got it all, but they still want something extra . . . they just can't name it.

"And men like you—miserable little men like you—marry them and spend their whole lives trying to satisfy them. And that makes them worse. It feeds their all-important ego. They think they can *have* it all. Everything! Just for the asking."

"She—she humiliates me," he mumbled. "Why? All right . . . I've given her everything. Everything I could ever afford. But she *still* humiliates me. That's—that's not fair."

"She humiliates you," she mocked gently. "And why? Because you've let her. You've let her get away with it. You've let her get away with it so often, it's become second nature to her." Then, in a slightly altered tone. "Why? In God's name, *why*? Listen to Keith. Listen to what Hellen had to say. You're the greatest thing since fishes learned to swim. You're Superman, himself. You won the war, single-handed. That's what I've been listening to all this time. Ron and Char Powell. God made *them*, then broke the mould. Then when I meet you—when I meet both of you—what do I find? What do I *really* find?"

"I'm—I'm sorry," he muttered.

"For heaven's sake! Stop being 'sorry' all the time. Bawl somebody out. Hit somebody, if necessary, just don't go through life being 'sorry'."

"You don't understand." The sigh was of resigned self pity. "You're young—newly married—you *can't* understand. It's possible . . ." He paused, and the tears over-flowed and began to run down his cheeks. "It's possible to fall *out* of love. You—you may not believe that. Now. Because you've just married Keith. To—to fall *out* of love with him. Impossible. That's what you think at the moment. That's what *I* once thought. Forever . . . see? Nobody—nobody like her. Never anybody likely to take her place. That's—that's what we *all* think. What we believe.

"B-but we're wrong, y'see. It's very easy. To fall *out* of love is a lot easier than falling in love. And—and you can't help yourself. You make excuses. All the excuses in the world. It's—it's because of this. Because of that. Because you're tired. Because *she's* tired. But it's all lies. All lies. Every excuse is a lie. And deep down you know it. You—you *know*. You won't admit it. At first you won't admit it. Never! It can't happen to *you*. But—but it *is* doing, and there's nothing you can do to stop it.

"It's not—it's not that you want to. Dear God, who *wants* to go through that sort of thing. You—you fight against it. But it's no good. The—the more you fight, the weaker you become. Well, y'do, don't you? The harder you fight and, if you can't win, the weaker you get. You—you start taking the easy way out. Pretending not to hear. Pretending you're going a bit deaf. Don't—don't hear things. That way, you can pretend not to have heard the hurtful things, and they don't seem to hurt as much. It—it didn't happen. She—she didn't say it. But she *did*, y'see. She did say it, and she *meant* it. But—but because you didn't hear—pretended not to have heard—what can you do? You can't answer back. You—you can't take offence. You can't do *anything*.

"Just—y'know—let her make a fool of you. Let her humiliate you. And—and it gets to be a habit. Falling out of love, bit at a time, it gets to be a habit. It's—it's—it's going to happen, anyway. There's nothing you can do to stop it. Nothing! So—y'know—let it happen. Don't fight it any more. Don't even try. Just—just put a face on for the outside world, but at home . . . When there's just the two of you. It's not worth it any more. Nothing. Nothing's worth it any more, because you're finished. Licked. And—and . . ."

He dropped his face into his hands, and his shoulders shook as the sobs tore through his whole body.

She stood up and quietly walked away. With sorrow rather than with disgust, even though she had sense enough to realise that some of the tears were alcoholic. She'd never seen a man cry before; even Keith, after the death of Hellen, had kept his misery a secret . . . if he'd wept (and, without doubt, he *had* wept) it had been in private and not for others to see.

And yet this man—this Ron she'd heard so much about—was not above cheap exhibitionism. To sob in front of a comparative stranger. To expose his private thoughts. To put on display the tattered wreck of a marriage, gone wrong because of his own weakness.

How could it be?

How could it make sense?

14

The Foolishness

KEITH tapped on the door and Char's voice called, "It isn't locked."

The tone was sharp and impatient and Keith wondered whether, after all, it was a mistake to try to make overtures as a first step towards bringing the annual party to normality.

Char was a bit of a handful. Always had been. Off the handle, at nothing, but not really *meaning* it. Violent likes, violent dislikes . . . for no logical reason. Christ, she'd been lucky, but she hadn't the simple gumption to realise it. Old Ron, there—three offices, a nice steady business and his own boss. Two grand sons—one going to be some sort of lawyer—the other in with his dad in the business and, in time, no doubt taking over. Clover, mate. That's what dear little Char was in. Up to the knees in clover, and too daft to know it.

"*It isn't locked!*"

This time the tone carried ill-tempered irritability.

Keith sighed, turned the knob and walked into the bedroom.

"If you think that little speech you made was going to . . ."

"Oh! I thought . . ."

They spoke together. She saw him through the dressing-table mirror at which she was sitting, brushing her hair. He saw her and blinked his momentary embarrassment; she was wearing only panties and bra; very thin, very abbreviated panties and a bra which only covered the lower part of her breasts.

She lowered the hairbrush, and said, "I thought it was that damn-fool husband of mine."

"I'm sorry. I—er—I didn't know you were . . ."

Again, they both spoke together.

She turned to face him and said, "Shut the door. It's not a peep-show. And you've seen me in a bikini enough times."

"Yes, I suppose so, but . . ."

"Shut the door, and stop behaving like a shocked curate, for God's sake."

He closed the door and walked farther into the room. Very gingerly, he lowered himself onto the edge of one of the twin beds.

"Well?" The question was accompanied by a tight, mocking smile.

"I . . ." He fumbled for words. "It's about downstairs. In the dining room."

"You mean The Powell Chat Show?"

"It—it was unnecessary. Uncalled for."

"What *I* said? Or what *he* said?"

"Both of you, really."

She tossed the hairbrush onto the other twin bed, stood up, followed it and sat down. She was less than a yard from him—much less than a yard—and, try as he might, he was aware of it. Aware of the hint of perfume. Aware of the tawny-coloured skin and the slim, cared-for figure. He was also aware that he'd had enough to drink . . . more than enough.

He cleared his throat, lowered his eyes and said, "I just don't want it spoiled, that's all."

"This annual jamboree?"

"It's more than that?"

"It was once," she admitted.

"It still is. And I don't want it ruined."

"There's a fly in the ointment." It was said bluntly but, strangely, with a certain amount of sadness.

"Ada?"

"She's not one of us, you know. She never can be."

"I—I don't see why."

"She didn't live through it. That's why."

"She understands."

"No." She shook her head. "Nobody 'understands'. They either know or they don't know. Even us, we're starting to forget."

"I'll not forget," he said softly.

"Oh, yes. Without Hellen there to remind you, you'll forget."

"Don't *you* remember?" he asked, and there was a degree of urgency in the question.

"Oh, yes." She sighed. "When I'm feeling particularly charitable, I look at him —at Ron, I mean—and I force myself to remember. But it's becoming increasingly difficult. He's changed so. Good God, even you can see he's changed. Nothing used to frighten him. Now, he's terrified of his own shadow. He's not the same man. He's not even a *man* any more."

"That's a lousy thing to say." But there was no real censure in the remark.

"It's a lousy world, Keith. You know that . . . better than any of us. This place. All this luxury. *You* couldn't afford it. *We'd* be pushed . . . and we're better off than you are. Jim can afford it. He can afford to foot the bill every year. He has the lolly. And he did *nothing*."

"It's his way of showing gratitude. It isn't necessary, but he insists."

"I wonder?" she mused gently.

"What?"

"Never mind. Enjoy your two days of make-believe. But *I* know and Emily knows. And Hellen knew."

"Can't we forget Hellen?" There was a pleading quality there. "Just for two days, can't we forget Hellen?"

"Can *you* forget Hellen?" she challenged softly.

"I—I try . . . sometimes," he breathed.

"Tell me." The tone was of near-academic interest. "I've often wondered. You and this new wife of yours. All men—come to that, all women—who marry more than once. Twice, three times, what have you. Do you *compare*?"

"I'm—I'm sorry. I don't . . ."

"In bed. Is there a silent comparison? Some sort of points system, perhaps?"

"No. Not a 'points system'." His voice was low and a little hoarse.

"But a comparison . . . surely?"

"I—I suppose so."

"Interesting." She picked up the hairbrush and began to tap the back of the brush against her bare thigh. Gently. Slowly, but rhythmically. In little more than a whisper, she said, "I once asked Hellen the same question, and she told me to mind my own damned business."

The implication behind the soft-spoken remark sank in, slowly. He raised his head and stared into her half-smiling face. The hairbrush continued its gentle, rhythmic slapping and the rounded thigh quivered slightly at each tap.

"That's—that's impossible," he choked. "That bloody ailment. She couldn't . . ."

"She didn't *always* have asthma." The smile widened, fractionally. "You were away from home a lot. Days at a time." A pause, then pointedly, "Are you claiming that you didn't have your moments of wild, illicit passion?"

"Not once," he groaned. "Dammit . . . *not once*."

"Bloody boring, isn't it?" she observed conversationally.

"Oh God!"

"That's what Hellen once said. 'It must be bloody boring.' To me, when I told her I'd been faithful to Ron. It shocked me at the time, but how right she was."

"You're . . ." He closed, then opened his eyes. "You're just being bitchy, aren't you? Lies. Telling deliberate lies to . . ."

"No, not lies." The hairbrush continued to slap. "I'm not telling lies, Keith. I'm removing blinkers. Yours and mine. I loved Hellen, like a sister. I didn't approve of her morals, but who was I to go around telling tales? The old slice-off-a-cut-loaf gag. That's the way *she* looked at it. Who was *I* to cause trouble?"

"Did she . . ." He swallowed. "Did she ever say who?"

"Not all. But—er—this new wife of yours has a brother, I think?"

He nodded dumbly.

"That one knew his way to the bedroom."

"Y'mean Ada . . ."

"No." She shook her head, and what might have been disappointment flickered in her eyes. "Not with *her* connivance. Not even with her knowledge . . . unfortunately."

"Unfortunately?" He looked puzzled.

"Keith." The hairbrush slapped. The thigh quivered. The voice was calm and unhurried. "I don't know why you came here . . ."

"To see you and Ron. To . . ."

"But, now you are here, you're not going away empty-handed. You're taking something with you, if it's only an experience."

"Look. I think I'd better . . ."

"You're also *leaving* an experience. Ron isn't a man any more. And that's what I need—what I've needed for a long time—a man. I've told you things I might never have told you. *Would* never have told you, whilever Hellen was alive." The free hand disappeared behind her back and the flimsy bra fell away. "Hellen was so right. It *is* bloody boring. And, just once, before it's too late—before I'm too old—I'm tossing my bonnet over a windmill."

"Please, Char. Don't tempt me. Don't . . ."

"Don't tell me you don't want to." Her eyes lowered themselves to stare brazenly at his crotch. "I'm a married woman. I can remember things. I can *see*. Stop wasting time, trying to talk yourself out of it."

"Char. It's not right. Ron might . . ."

"Lock the door, Keith. Lock the door. I'll send Ron running if he arrives."

"Char, I don't *want* to."

"Liar."

She threw the hairbrush onto the bed, stood up, gave a wriggle and the panties fell to her ankles. She stepped from them, and she had the body of a twenty-year-old. She was something he'd dreamed about while Hellen—dear, sweet, two-timing Hellen—had been too ill to be a true wife.

"Char." The name seemed to choke him. "It's not right. I'm . . ."

"I'm not talking about loving." The words came from behind clenched teeth. "I'm not even talking about kissing—love-play—any of that crap. I'm talking about honest-to-God screwing. Lock that bloody door, pick the bed, drop your pants and screw me."

15

Booze Talk

NIGHT PORTERS are a breed apart. They see, then forget, the worst in their fellow-men . . . and sometimes in their fellow-women. Beyond a certain o'clock they take over the responsibility for the smooth-running of a complete hotel. Even a hotel like The Cave. They are at the beck and call of every guest. The management, the waiters, the kitchen staff, the bar staff have all retired. Only the Night Porter remains on duty; only *he* panders to the whimsical needs of anything up to a hundred and fifty guests.

Some clown wants an early call and has forgotten to notify the desk before retiring. No sweat; ring down and the Night Porter will fix things. Some howling kid needs gripe water at three in the morning. Not to worry; gripe water it is, with the minimum of delay. Anything. From an ambulance to a bed-companion; from a postage stamp to a new bulb for the bedside lamp; from black coffee to a trans-Atlantic telephone call. The Night Porter is unique. The others only *think* they're indispensable.

Jim Bathurst held out his glass, and the Night Porter dutifully measured out yet one more double-whisky.

"C'mon, have one with me."

"No, thank you, sir. It's as much as my job's worth."

"Who the hell's gonna know?"

"If there's an emergency, sir. I have to attend. One of the guests smells whisky on my breath and complains to the manager. I'd be out, sir. Thank you, but no."

"What a bloody job!" murmured Jim.

They were in the hall lounge of the hotel; within sight of the entrance and within easy reach of the telephones. The Night Porter didn't mind the company of this booze-swilling guest and, although the bar was long-closed, experience made it no problem for him to keep a mental tally of the number of doubles being poured.

It happened like this sometimes. The guests were always right and, if a guest felt like drinking the night away, that was okay. The appropriate stuff was always available.

When he allowed himself to think along such lines—which wasn't often—the Night Porter tended towards the opinion that, with some people, money equated with stupidity. After all, they'd paid (or were going to pay) for a comfortable bed, with all mod cons, and then figured they were missing out on things by crawling into that bed and enjoying a good night's sleep. They had to be awake. They had to be doing something . . . even if it was only spending more money getting as tight as a tick. But it was *their* money and, if that's what they wanted that, too, could be catered for.

"You in the war, old son?" asked Jim.

"No, sir. I was a schoolboy at the time."

"That a fact?"

"I was an evacuee."

"That a fact?" repeated Jim. "Where to?"

"From Birmingham to Morecambe, actually."

"Morecambe?"

"Yes, sir."

"Just up the coast?"

"That's right, sir. I never returned to Birmingham."

"That a fact?" Jim seemed to favour the three-word question.

"From school to the hotel trade. I've been in the hotel trade ever since."

"Fetching and carrying all your life?"

"I enjoy the job, sir."

Jim downed whisky, then said, "You missed out on things, son."

"Yes, sir." The Night Porter wasn't there to argue.

"All this modern stuff." Jim waved his free arm. "Jet this, jet that, jet the other. Phantoms. Jump Jets. Jumbo jets. The bloody Concorde. All a lot of balls."

"Yes, sir."

"Gimme a prop kite, every time."

"Yes, sir."

"With a prop kite, you know where you *stand*."

"Yes, sir."

"Ever been up in a Lanc?"

"No, sir. I can't say I . . ."

"No, you wouldn't. Too young. Finest aeroplane ever designed, old lad."

"Yes, sir."

"Bloody *marvellous*!"

"So I'm told."

"*I'm* telling you. I flew the bloody things."

"Indeed, sir."

"On ops. During the war. The *real* war."

"Yes, sir."

"Up the Ruhr, eh? Flack like bloody confetti. Night fighters chasing you all the way home." He finished the whisky and held the glass for a re-fill. "But we warmed the Germans' arses. By God, we warmed the Germans' arses."

"So I've read, sir." The Night Porter poured another double.

"A great time, old son," pronounced Jim solemnly. "We *enjoyed* it."

"I—er—I don't think I would have, sir." The Night Porter braved himself to contradict a guest.

"Eh? Course you would."

"I—er—perhaps so, sir. Perhaps I would."

"Men, lad. Men. Not piss-arsed ninnies they are today."

"If you say so, sir," sighed the Night Porter.

"I had a crew. You've met some of 'em. Ron and Keith."

"Mr. Parkinson. Mr. Powell."

"Men, lad," repeated Jim. "Salt of the earth. Get a crew—a good crew—they never let you down. *Never*! Like the old Lanc. *She'd* never let you down, either. Flack. Fighters. She took 'em all on. No bloody trouble. No trouble at all."

Upstairs, Emily closed the Agatha Christie, turned off the bedside light and settled down to sleep. She knew her husband. He'd have found a listener. Keith, perhaps. Or Ron. Anybody. And he'd be re-fighting his war—re-flying his operations—and that was *him* happy till dawn.

16

Shame

KEITH PARKINSON knotted the cord of his pyjamas as he walked from the bathroom. His hair was unruly and still damp from the shower and, without the "wings" of carefully positioned grey he looked his age and not as consciously "handsome and experienced". As he reached for the pyjama jacket his wife stirred in the other bed, opened her eyes and watched him for a moment.

"What time is it?" she asked sleepily.

"Er . . ." He consulted the wrist-watch on the bedside table. "Going up to three. Go back to sleep."

"Are you drunk?" There was no hint of criticism in the question.

"No. Of course not."

"Where have you been?" She gradually became more awake. "Where have you been, till this time?"

"Out," he lied.

"I didn't see you."

"What?"

"I went for a walk, remember? I didn't see you."

"Oh! Er—no—you wouldn't. Just a brisk walk round the hotel grounds. I didn't go near the prom."

"Ron followed me," she yawned. Then, quite suddenly, she sat up in bed and said, "I could smoke a cigarette."

"How d'you mean? 'Ron followed you'? Y'mean he tried to pick you up?"

"Good Lord, no!" She stared. "Why on earth should he?"

"He always—y'know—fancied himself," he lied. "Still waters. That sort of thing. A bit of a lady's man, at heart."

"You know, I'd never have thought . . ."

"You don't have to. Now, you know."

He fumbled cigarettes from a packet alongside the wrist-watch, and silently called himself a louse. Such lies! And about Ron, too. The steadiest man on two legs. Always had been. And *he* was calling him *that*.

He lighted the cigarettes and handed one to her. He moved the ash-tray slightly, in order that they could share it more easily, then he sat on the edge of his own bed.

She inhaled, blew smoke, then said, "He's a sick man, Keith."

"Sick?" He almost snapped the word out.

"Yes. Unhappy sick. Miserable." She hesitated, then added, "I left him sitting on one of the promenade seats, crying his heart out."

"Good God!"

"He needs treatment. I'm sure of it."

"Of all the . . ." He closed his mouth and drew deeply on the cigarette.

He made no move to switch on a bedside lamp. The light from the bathroom was sufficient. Maybe *too* sufficient. She *had* to know. It *had* to show. Christ Almighty, a man couldn't come straight from a . . .

"I think you should have a quiet word with him," she said.

"Eh?"

"Advise him. *Somebody* should. He's your friend. There's something terribly wrong with him."

"It's none of our business."

"Keith, he's your friend. He's not some . . ."

"All right! It's that cow of a wife of his." He thrashed around, reaching for straws in an attempt to prevent complete submersion in the choking mire of his guilt. "Downstairs. Earlier. You were there. She'll do anything—say anything—*anything*!"

"It wasn't important. Ron made things worse by . . ."

"Not *important*!"

"A dirty-postcard remark. For goodness sake, we're not . . ."

"That's *her*. The way she thinks." His voice rose as he threw guilt in all directions. "She's foul. She's just a sex-starved, dirty-minded . . ."

"Keith. Quieten down. Don't shout. Strangers might hear and wonder what on earth . . ."

"I'm sorry." Then in a broken voice, "Oh God, I'm sorry," but his misery wasn't because of the volume of his voice.

The silence was heavy with strange recriminations. Keith's self-recrimination, made worse by Char's mischievous accusation of Hellen's past infidelities. He didn't want to believe, but couldn't disbelieve. Other than because it was the truth, why else should the revelation have been made? It was possible. More than possible. Easy, in fact. For years, his work had taken him away from home. The opportunity had been there. And if the *opportunity*?

"Your—your brother . . ." he muttered.

"Wally? What about him?"

"What sort of a man is he?"

"He . . ." She hesitated, then said, "He's not the worst man in the world. Why?"

"Or the best?"

"No. I don't think even *he'd* claim that. But why do you ask?"

"Just that . . ."

He couldn't bring himself to voice the question. To spread the guilt a little; not make it less—nothing could make it *less*—but at least show that others, too, carried guilt.

"What about Wally?" she asked in a puzzled tone.

"Nothing. I was just thinking, that's all."

"You're in a funny mood," she accused gently.

"Yeah . . . aren't I?"

'Funny'. By God that was one way of putting it. 'Funny'—peculiar. 'Funny'—ha—ha. But neither of those, this time. 'Funny'—conscience-stricken. 'Funny'—ashamed. 'Funny'—disillusioned. About Hellen, and about that damn brother-in-law of his but, most of all, about *himself*. Christ, hadn't he given Char the big stick? And wouldn't she use it? Wouldn't she *just*!

In a soft, unsteady voice, he said, "In hell's name, why did you marry me?"

"Wha-at?" Her jaw dropped and her eyes opened.

"What am I? Just what the hell *am* I?"

"You're Keith Parkinson. You're the man I . . ."

"I'm a hawker." The bitterness turned the tone ugly. "In flash language I'm what they like to call 'a representative'. A bloody commercial traveller. That's all. That's all I'll ever be. All the mucky 'commercial traveller' jokes . . . I'm part of 'em. They may be true. How the hell do *you* know?

"I hawk jewellery. Not even *real* jewellery. Imitation. Paste. Junk. I hawk it all over the blasted country. 'Yes, sir. No, sir. Three bags full, sir.' That's my stock-in-trade. I have to sell the bloody stuff, otherwise we go hungry. Otherwise we don't eat. Even the damn car. *I* couldn't afford a car. Not even a small car, much less a Cortina. That's what I am, girl. A travelling salesman, hawking trash."

"I'm not a 'girl'," she said tightly. "I'm your wife."

"That could make you a bigger fool than I am." He squashed what was left of the cigarette into the ash-tray and reached for the pyjama jacket.

"What's got into you?" she asked, and there was a touch of anger there now.

"Honesty." He shrugged his arms through the jacket sleeves. "This place, maybe. All this yearly two-days-of-luxury crap. Just don't take it seriously, that's all. Don't take *anything* seriously."

In a single movement, he flung the bedclothes open, rolled between them, pulled them up to his neck and curled with his back to her. He didn't even say, "Goodnight".

She smoked the cigarette, watched his rumpled hair and felt sad. This was a Keith she hadn't known before. A Keith who, for some secret reason, wouldn't "let her inside". It hurt. It hurt her more than it angered her, but she had wisdom enough to know that he, too, was hurting.

She finished the cigarette, squashed the tipped end into the ash-tray, then left her bed to switch off the bathroom light. Men! Something had gone wrong. They'd had a row, perhaps. Keith—Jim—even Ron, perhaps—some silly drunken argument, in which offence had been taken. What else? Like little boys, fighting over nothing. And, come morning, it would be all forgotten and they'd be buddies again.

Nevertheless, it took her more than an hour to quieten her mind enough for sleep to come.

Keith didn't stir . . . but *he* didn't sleep at all.

17

Dawn

AT Lytham St. Annes each new day creeps up from behind; it fingers the rooftops first, while leaving the surface of the sea in darkness. It is the reverse side of the coin of magnificent sunsets, and the pre-dawn chill rarely leaves the promenade until the long shadows of the sea-front hotels have shrunk, then disappeared. The night can have been warm and clear—a night for strollers, a night for lovers—but that hour before dawn brings gooseflesh and shivers to all but the hardy.

The patrolling constables know this, but it is a small enough price to pay for policing such a place.

Nevertheless, the duo of uniformed officers in the patrol car were none too pleased when they spotted the lone figure hunched on the promenade seat. It was warm and cosy in the patrol car, they'd been on duty since ten o'clock, and within the next thirty minutes they were due back at the station, with the promise of a welcome bed awaiting. An arrest would mean paperwork and general fannying around, and they'd be lucky if they were away before seven-thirty . . . on top of which there might even be the inconvenience of a court appearance.

"Have we seen him?" asked the driver pointedly.

"Better safe than sorry." The officer doing observer duty sighed. "He might be an important lift. Some of the villains still circulating need pulling in."

"So be it," said the driver resignedly.

He turned from the road and drove onto one of the Lytham Green car parks, dousing the lights of the vehicle as he did so. As the car slowed to a silent halt, the observer radioed in the information that they were going "off the air" pending enquiries. They left the car together, closing the doors quietly, the driver pocketing the ignition key as they did so. Then they walked silently across the grass to the bench.

The observer stood behind the man on

the seat, ready to move if necessary. Too many coppers had been nobbled recently. It behove any right-thinking constable not to take chances. The driver walked to the front of the man, and spoke.

"Now, sir. Mind telling us what you're doing here?"

"Eh? Oh! Ah!" The man was startled. He'd had his eyes closed. "I—I must have dropped off."

"Been here all night, have you?"

"Er—yes—I suppose so."

"No overcoat? No mac? Bit cold for sleeping rough, isn't it?"

"I'm—er—I'm not sleeping rough. I'm . . ."

"What name is it?" asked the driver.

"What?"

"Your name, and your address, please."

"Powell. Ronald Powell. I'm—er—I'm not doing anything wrong, am I?"

"If not, you've nothing to worry about," said the driver, enigmatically. "What's your home address?"

Ron told them.

The driver said, "Have you proof of that?"

"My driving licence?" suggested Ron. "But I'm . . ."

"That'll do. You have it on you?"

Ron made a move towards the inside pocket of his jacket. The observer stepped closer and gripped a shoulder. Ron jerked round and stared, frightened, at the second officer.

"Just easy," said the observer politely. "The driving licence. That's all."

"Of—of course. It's in my wallet."

"Okay, just the wallet."

Ron produced the wallet, and the driver shone a torch in his face. They knew their job. They were as wary as cats on strange ground. The driver took the offered driving licence, and read the details.

Politely, he said, "You haven't signed it, sir."

"Haven't I?"

"I'll take it with me. Check up. It won't take long."

"Look, I'm . . ."

But the driver was already walking away, across the grass to the parked patrol car. The observer came from behind the bench and stood looking down at the frightened

Ron. He, too, had a torch, and the beam danced between Ron's face and hands.

"Just sit there, sir," he said. "Once we've checked. If you're in the clear, that's all we need to know."

"In the—in the clear?"

"We have to know. It's our job." He concentrated the torch on the red-rimmed eyes, and Ron squinted as the beam filled his whole vision. "Been here all night, you say?"

"I'm—I'm staying at The Cave."

"You don't say." The observer obviously didn't believe him.

"I—I came for a walk. I just sat down —y'know—to think."

"To think?"

"I must have dropped off."

"With a nice warm bed in The Cave?" The polite mockery wasn't offensive.

"Sounds silly, doesn't it?" Ron managed the ghost of a sad smile.

"A bit unusual," admitted the observer.

"God, it's cold." Ron shivered and pulled the collar of his jacket higher.

"That's what makes it sound so silly," said the observer. Then, "Are you wanted anywhere?"

"I—I beg your pardon?"

"Wanted? Is there a warrant out for you?"

"Good God, no! I've already said . . ."

"I know. The Cave Hotel. We'll check that, too, when my mate gets back." He paused, then added, "If you *are* wanted, he'll know."

"I'm not. I swear."

"No need to swear, sir. We'll *know*."

"Will he—will he be long?"

"Not more than a couple of minutes."

"I'm so *cold*."

Ron made to push his hands into the pockets of his jacket.

"Hold it!" The observer stopped being polite.

"I—I just want to warm my hands. That's all."

"Link them behind your neck, please," said the observer. "Just till I make sure."

Ron obeyed. The observer watched the hands as he leaned down and patted each jacket pocket in turn. Then, to be doubly sure, he dipped his hand into each pocket. He brought nothing out; merely double-checked on the initial frisking.

He smiled and said, "Okay, sir. Put your

hands into your jacket pockets if you think that might help."

"Thank you."

Ron sat, silently fighting the chill. He hunched his shoulders and wondered what the devil might come next.

Tentatively, he said, "What am I supposed to have done?"

"Nothing . . . as yet."

"I mean, why pick on *me*?"

"You're the only one around." The observer chuckled quietly. "We haven't 'picked' on you. It's what we're paid for. Anything unusual . . . we have to make sure."

"If—if I'd done anything wrong, I'd have run away."

"Not far." The observer moved his head. "We have a car. *We're* not restricted to roads. The grass, the promenade . . . you wouldn't have run far."

"Oh!"

He sat there and shivered as the cold seeped deeper. He tried to remember. Why? Why had he stayed out here all night? What had he said? He'd said *something*—he'd said a lot, to a woman who was almost a stranger—but how much? What had he told her? How *much*? He'd cracked up, he could remember cracking up. Not that it mattered, he supposed. Not that *anything* mattered any more. Only Char. What Char might say. What a scene she might—*would*—make. And he hadn't *meant* to stay out on the promenade all night.

"He's—he's taking a long time," he said.

"Not long," replied the observer, flatly. "Just checking."

Beyond the railing the wavelets rippled over pebbles and shingle. A hissing noise, which rose and fell. Like the audience at an old-time melodrama. Hissing the villain. And he was the villain.

Dear God, the name. "Powell". Hundreds of "Powells". Thousands. There *had* to be a "Powell' the police were looking for. Somebody called "Powell". There *had* to be a "Powell". And the Police Computer. He'd read about it—this Police Computer—housed in Hendon, he thought. But a computer, and computers made mistakes. They made big mistakes. Massive mistakes. And he'd been out here all night. Alone. No alibi. It was possible, more than possible . . .

"Look, I haven't done anything wrong," he said urgently.

"In that case, you've nothing to worry about."

It was like talking to a wall. This man had no feelings. No compassion. Like—like Char, *worse* than Char.

"Am I under arrest?" he asked desperately.

"No."

"In that case . . ." He swallowed. "In that case, I could go back to the hotel and you couldn't stop me."

"It wouldn't be a wise thing to do."

"Why? Why wouldn't it be a wise thing to do. If I'm not under arrest . . ."

"What are you getting excited about?"

"What?"

"What are you getting worried about? If you haven't done anything, what's the panic?"

"I'm—I'm not . . ."

"You *are*." The observer glanced to his right. "Anyway, we'll soon know."

The driver approached across the grass.

"Nothing known," he said, and sounded mildly disappointed. He handed the driving licence back to Ron and said, "Get it signed, as soon as possible, sir."

"Thank you." Ron stood up and continued, "It's all right, if I go back to . . ."

"We'll come with you," interrupted the observer.

"For God's sake! It's a class hotel."

The observer said, "That's why."

"If I walk in there with a police escort, they'll—they'll think . . ."

"We're going with you," said the observer. "Just to be sure."

Ron walked slowly towards The Cave Hotel, flanked by the two officers. Their presence made him feel guilty. Just them *being* there. But, as he'd discovered, they were beyond argument. They were doing a job. *Their* job. Objectively, he should have been pleased; pleased that taxes and rates were being conscientiously earned. *Subjectively* he felt outraged; that simply because he'd spent the night on a promenade bench, he was being treated like a criminal.

As they approached the entrance he saw Jim and the Night Porter through the windows of the entrance lounge. He stopped, and the two officers halted, one on each side of him.

"Well?" asked the observer, suspiciously.

"That man." Ron nodded towards the windows. "Talking to the porter. I'm with his party. Jim Bathurst, that's his name. I was his navigator during the war. *He* knows me. We're here together. Six of us. Three husbands, three wives. He can vouch for me."

"You're laughing tin hats then, aren't you?"

"Ask him to come out here," pleaded Ron. "Tell him. Tell him who I am, and ask him to come out. Don't—don't take me into the hotel, as if I was a . . ." He looked at the observer, and said, "*Please*!"

The observer hesitated, then shrugged and walked up the shallow steps to the entrance.

It wasn't *quite* as Ron would have liked it to have been. Jim came out and cleared away all last doubts in the minds of the officers. Of course he did. But things were said. Silly things. Embarrassing things. "Sat on a form all night, you *what*? Oh, all right. Tell it to Char. I'll make out I believe you. On the tiles, eh? Chance for a bit of spare, while you're able. Don't blame you—don't get me wrong—I'm not *blaming* you . . . for myself I prefer booze. But, Christ, you'd better have a neater yarn than that when Char sees you. Tell her you've been with me. I'll tip the Night Porter. He'll back you."

And, at last, he was allowed to free himself from the grinning constables and Jim's ridiculous insinuations. To make his way to the lift, and *not* be treated like a criminal or a hellrake.

18

Constitutionals

THE average Englishman on holiday does things he would never do at any other time of the year. Especially is this so when he (or she) is holidaying at a pleasant, seaside resort like Lytham St. Annes. At home, he crawls from bed at the last moment, wanders to the bathroom, is still half-asleep as he dresses, totters downstairs, sips instant coffee and chews moodily at a piece of toast, then leaves for his place of business. It takes him until mid-morning to slough off the daily irritation of *having* to leave the comfort of his bedroom.

But when he *hasn't*—when he's on holiday—he's up with the sun, washed, shaved, dressed and away. The morning, pre-breakfast constitutional—the brisk-walk-on-the-prom-first-thing syndrome—is part of the holiday. Especially is this so at Lytham St. Annes. The resort caters for that type of person, and the promenade is designed to give an early-morning feeling of freedom and fresh air.

Guests from the various hotels and lodging houses mix with residents in this mildly idiotic search for instant health. The former tend to favour the tarmac of the promenade walk, within easy sight of the unaccustomed sea. The latter go for the long, broad stretch of the Green, if only to allow their companion dogs to bark and scamper and generally give vent to their canine good-to-be-alive feeling.

And it was (it must be admitted) a glorious, walk-on-the-prom morning. The sun had topped the roofs. The sea was sparkling like a scene from a telly ad. There was little breeze; just enough to waft the tang of seaweed up from the shore-line.

Emily wore a lightweight, loose-fitting coat and a headscarf. She carried a slim walking-cane. She, of them all, made no pretence of ignoring the approach of age. She walked slowly and deliberately and, every fifty yards or so, she paused to gaze out to sea.

As she paused, for the fourth time, Keith

joined her and leaned with his elbows on the railing.

"A beautiful morning, Keith," she smiled.

"Yeah." He stared at the distant horizon.

"Sleep well?"

"No." There was a pause, then, "Not at all."

"Really?" She turned to look at his face more closely. "No, it's fairly obvious. You look ill."

"I'm not ill," he assured her quietly.

"Too much to drink last night, perhaps."

"No."

She accepted the negative answer without comment, turned to face the sea again and waited.

"Emily . . ." he began, then stopped.

"Those ships." She raised her cane and pointed, sweeping the cane to encompass the arc of three merchant vessels moving slowly along the sky-line. "I wonder. Are they making for Liverpool or the mouth of the Ribble?"

"You've—er—always been the 'mother figure'. Of the six of us, you've always been the—sort of—*mater familias*, as it were."

"It would be nice to know." She lowered the cane. "If they're making for the Ribble, that means Preston."

"Being Jim's wife, and Jim being the skipper. That's really what I mean."

"Does Preston mean Manchester? The Manchester Ship Canal. Does it link Preston and Manchester? I really should know more about these things."

"Emily, I'm talking to you," he said quietly.

"Of course you are." She smiled. "So far, you've politely called me an old woman —which I don't dispute—and Jim's wife, which we both know to be true."

"Last night . . ." It almost choked him, then it came out with a rush. "I made love to Char."

"Made love?" She continued to watch the ships.

"You know what I mean."

"You used the word 'love'."

"All right," he muttered desperately. "We had intercourse."

"I think the word you're seeking is 'lust', isn't it?"

"If—if you like."

"Isn't it?" she insisted.

"Yes. All right. Blind, bloody lust."

"Oh, dear." She sighed. "Ron *will* be cross when he gets to know."

"You—you think . . ." He moistened his lips, and tasted the hint of salt on their surface. "You think she'll tell him?"

"Are you naive enough to think she *won't*?"

"Oh, my God!" He gazed out to sea, but without looking at anything. He groaned, "Dammit. I didn't want to do it. I really *didn't* want to do it."

"Somebody held a gun to your head," she suggested mildly.

"I—I beg your pardon?"

"As you say." She turned and walked slowly along the side of the promenade railing. "I'm an old woman . . ."

"No!" He caught up with her, and fell in step. "I didn't mean to . . ."

"At least elderly. Old enough to know that 'not wanting to' and 'wishing you hadn't' isn't quite the same thing."

"What the hell do I do?" he groaned. Then hurriedly, "You won't tell Ada?"

"I won't tell *anybody*."

"Can I—can I talk about it?" he pleaded. "Christ, I've got to tell *somebody*. Please . . . can I talk about it?"

"I have perfectly good hearing," she said calmly. "If you talk, I'll listen. Beyond that, I make no promises."

They strolled south, along the promenade. He talked; the gabbled mixed-up sentences of a man worried out of his mind; the whole story, intermingled with excuses which even *he* knew weren't *really* excuses. Her face showed no emotion. Not even real interest. She kept glancing out to sea, as if checking the progress of the three merchant vessels. They reached the end of the promenade, turned and walked slowly back north. He ended his story. Abruptly. Like the last of the water disappearing down the plug of a bath. Then, still in step, they walked slowly for another twenty yards or so. She turned, then stopped to watch the shimmering sea and the three vessels.

He joined her at the railing, and muttered, "Well?"

"Should you tell Ada? That's what you're asking, isn't it?"

"One of the things." He nodded.

"Hellen didn't tell *you*." She squinted

out to sea, as if trying to identify one of the vessels.

"That's not the same . . ."

"You stayed in love with her. You were happy. Char knew about the extra-marital relationships. So did I."

"You?"

"From Char. Then from Hellen herself. We all three got pretty drunk some years back. A lot of all-girls-together talk. We all three knew."

"Christ, you must have been laughing at . . ."

"I don't laugh at those things, Keith." She turned to face him. "Love. Honour. Obey. I said those words a long time ago and meant them. They're as important now as ever they were."

"I'm—I'm sorry," he mumbled.

"Maybe that's why I'm the 'old lady' of the group. Old-fashioned ideas . . . that sort of thing."

"Emily. I—I . . ." He moved his hands, helplessly. "I love you. Not—not *that* way. Y'know . . ."

"More like a mother," she taunted gently. "Okay. Motherly advice. Don't *forget* last night. Use it as a warning. Just don't let it grow into a habit."

"That's not what I'm . . ."

"And don't tell Ada. It might be good for *your* soul. It could tear *hers* from its moorings. Stay a little unhappy. Live with the guilt. Sharing it doesn't halve it, that's a come-on. Let your new wife love you. Don't kill it before it has time to grow."

"And Char?" he asked timorously.

Before answering she began the slow walk back towards the hotel. Her cane tap-tapping on the tarmac. Her carriage proud and certain. He walked alongside her as they spoke in little more than murmurs.

"Can you keep a secret?" she asked.

"Of course."

"No gloating? No 'getting your own back', because you think you've been seduced?"

"I promise."

"Char took Ron on the rebound," she said calmly. "He proposed to *me* first and I refused. He couldn't have me, so he had to settle for Char." They walked a few yards in silence. "That to a woman like Char—to the sort of woman Char's become—is a skeleton in the cupboard. Something

I've no doubt she tries to forget, but can't. I'll have a quiet word with her. Blackmail her a little." She turned her head seawards. "Y'know, I'm inclined to think those ships are making for Liverpool. They'd be turning inshore if they were moving into the mouth of the Ribble."

"Emily. I—y'know—I don't know how I can . . ."

"It's nice walking on the promenade, don't you think?" she interrupted. "Very bracing. It sharpens the appetite for breakfast. By the way, Jim's in the Sauna . . . so one of the staff tells me. Steaming the all-night booze from his pores, no doubt. You might get word to him. Breakfast is at nine. I'd like him to be there."

19

Breakfast

AS in most top class hotels, breakfast in The Cave is a strangely sedate meal. The noise and laughter—the chatter and the let down hair—of the previous evening's dinner is absent. Guests enter the dining room quietly; almost on tip-toe. Occasionally, there is a silently nodded greeting to fellow-guests, as they thread their way through the tables, but the talk is in little more than whispers.

The ladies seize the opportunity to show off their latest new season finery. The men wear open-necked shirts and cravat-tied silk scarves as a defiant gesture to their rest-of-the-year collars and ties. There is, therefore, a peculiar relaxation about this first meal of the day; a relaxation which is at once timidly cheerful and shy, but which is kept under strict control and must never rid itself of impeccable manners.

The staff, too, join in this genteel façade. From the receptionists to the hall porters, from the dining room staff to the white-coated bedroom cleaners, there is this smoothly-moving quietness. Speed, without rush. No clatter. No under-the-breath humming of popular melodies. Even the housekeeper keeps her chained bunch of master-keys tucked firmly away in a pocket to prevent unnecessary jangling.

It was the same at the oval table.

The men—none of whom had slept that night—looked slightly baggy-eyed. Ron's eyes were also red-rimmed and Keith, although pale-faced, looked more relaxed and showed greater attention to the wants of Ada than he had previously. Jim, on the other hand—and apart from the under-eyed bagginess—looked almost impossibly healthy and alive for a man who'd consumed more than a bottle of Scotch instead of sleeping. An hour in the Sauna, followed by an ice-cold shower, had made his skin tingle and chased away any hint of hangover.

Of the women, Emily looked the brightest; she had that pseudo-innocent, cat-that's-nicked-the-top-of-the-milk look, and it balanced, to perfection, the slightly tight-lipped expression of Char's. Ada looked a little pale—she hadn't slept much either—but was obviously pleasantly surprised at (and appreciative of) Keith's concern for her comfort and welfare.

For all of thirty minutes they ate in comparative silence. Normal pleasantries and requests were made, of course—"Pass the salt, please." "Anybody want more kippers?" "Marmalade, anybody? Lemon, orange or lime?" that sort of thing—but it was only when Jim drained the last of his tea that the day's activities were touched upon.

He pushed the crockery a fraction of an inch away from him, dabbed his lips with his napkin, then spoke to the whole table.

"Six o'clock, this evening," he said, and grinned at the thought of things to come. "That's when we all get together again. The shindig starts at seven . . . prompt. No late take-offs. As always, it's in the Cavern Room. Ada . . ." He beamed at the new member of the group. "You're in for a treat, girl." Ada returned the smile, and he continued. "Any of you want to stay here—anybody wants to have lunch here—that's fine. Everything's fixed. But till six o'clock, you can all play circuits and bumps wherever you like. I have a spot of business to see to, the usual thing when we have these parties, but don't worry, I'll be back in time for take-off. All clear?"

Keith said, "I think Ada would like to see Fleetwood."

"See Fleetwood and die!"

Char said, "I don't think *we'll* go far. A little shopping, perhaps."

In a voice with a certain amount of needle, Ron added, "We've no great choice . . . unless Char can talk somebody else into driving us around in a van."

"The taxi *has* been invented," she snapped.

"That's it, then." Jim smoothed the rising hackles. "You're on your own till six o'clock but, at six o'clock, no absentees allowed."

20

Golden Mile

"WHEN we were kids," reminisced Keith. "Dick and me. I can *just* remember it. The Golden Mile—the old, original Golden Mile—with more sharks to the square foot than in any ocean in the world . . ."

He cruised the Cortina slowly north along the Blackpool promenade road, with the Tower looming nearer on the right. Ada had never seen Blackpool before. Never seen anything *like* Blackpool. Never seen a whole town geared solely for holiday-making. Never seen so many gaudily-painted frontages whose only aim was to take as much as possible for as little as possible.

"It wasn't like this in the old days. Christ, this is *neat*. This is *organised*. In those days, it was all open-air. Roundabouts. Roll-a-ball games. Peep-shows.

Rock stalls. There was a rock stall every few yards, and they made the stuff there, for you to see. Slinging it on a hook, pulling and throwing it. Then fixing the lettering before rolling it out, by hand, while you were watching . . ."

The truth was, she didn't like it too much. The smell of frying sausages and hot onions from the hot-dog stands smothered what scent of sea air there might have been. The brash invitation of the "fun palace", with its row after row of slot machines and its architectural tartiness was to her visually overpowering. And the crowds! Why, in God's name, there wasn't a fatal road accident every hundred yards or so seemed a miracle.

"And the gimmick shows. Bearded ladies, two-headed calves, vicars living in barrels, real-life mermaids, people fasting almost to death in glass-fronted booths. I tell you. If it was out of the ordinary, it was on the Golden Mile . . . especially if it was in bad taste. All jammed together, in one great mix-up . . ."

And the tram cars. Rolling, rattling, clanking and (or so it seemed) nose to tail, thundering north and south on their left. Too close for comfort. Too near to feel quite *safe*.

"And see here? Lewis's. That's where the Palace was. It used to be the Tower, the Winter Gardens and the Palace. And the piers, of course. Three super ballrooms. And shows. *On With The Show* on the North Pier. Always *On With The Show*. And variety at the Palace. I can remember when . . ."

"I don't want to," she interrupted breathlessly. Almost panic-stricken.

"Eh?" He came from the past and stared at her.

"It's . . ." She clenched her fists in her lap. "I don't like it here, Keith. It's too noisy. Too many people."

"Oh!"

"It frightens me a little."

"They're only enjoying themselves," he said in a soothing tone. "They won't *hurt* you. It's their way, that's all."

"Is Fleetwood like this?" she whispered.

"Good Lord, no. *Nowhere's* like this. Only Blackpool."

She took a deep breath, then said, "Let's

get out of here. Let's get to Fleetwood. This is . . . Let's get out of it, Keith. Please."

21

Pleasure Beach

MULTIPLY the Golden Mile tenfold, then double it and double it again, and you end up with something approximating the Pleasure Beach. Ask the American visitors. In World War II, when the Yanks arrived by the thousand, the Pleasure Beach took their breath away . . . and it has more than doubled since then. Americans still come and are dumbfounded. By comparison their much vaunted Coney Island is a small collection of painted junk. It is the greatest, most concentrated collection of switch-backs, rides, stalls, ferris wheels, side-shows, shooting galleries, fun houses and general funfair paraphernalia on the face of the earth. That first drop on the Big Dipper takes *everybody's* stomach to the back of their throat. The Grand National sets *two* cars off at the same time, and they race up and down on twin tracks, riding dips and climbs no less hair-raising, as they thunder and sway towards the "Winning Post" at the end of the ride. If you feel so disposed, you can see a spectacular on ice; confound yourself in a hall of mirrors; eat at the biggest restaurant in town; totter along a "cakewalk"; have your skirts lifted high above your head by a sudden jet of warm air; eat ice cream and candy floss until you're sick; be whirled around until gravity seems no longer to have meaning. Anything. Everything. It's all there. Bigger, brasher, more terrifying than anywhere else in the world.

People do not "visit" the Pleasure Beach. They go for the day. They go with their wallets thick with notes . . . and they leave with a few coins jangling in their pockets.

Nor is it called a beach for nothing. Despite its present well-made roads and walkways, it began on sand. On the dunes, on the outskirts of Blackpool where fortune-tellers and a few roundabout owners made their pitches. Thereafter, it grew . . . and grew . . . and grew. Millions of pounds were spent, millions of pounds were made, millions of pounds were lost. Without the Pleasure Beach, Blackpool would be like a man with only one arm. Indeed, it wouldn't *be* Blackpool.

Jim and Emily Bathurst strolled among the crowds milling between the countless booths and stalls. Emily knew, from past experience, that Jim wouldn't (couldn't!) pass the Pleasure Beach without a quick look-in and a wander around. They'd parked the car on a private—almost secret—park belonging to the man responsible for one of the main rides, and a man who'd been a longtime friend of Jim's. And now they walked and were jostled along one of the tarmac ways which criss-crossed the massive, permanent fairground.

"Hang about a bit."

Jim peeled off and made his way to a shooting gallery. Emily sighed and followed. She knew her man. Somebody was in for a shock.

The stallholder smiled a welcome and spieled, "Now, sir. Fancy your chance? Show the little lady what a dead-eyed-Dick you are?"

"That?" Jim pointed.

"That" was the star prize. It took pride of place among all the general junk making up the minor prizes. It was a teddy bear; a teddy bear as big as a normal five-year-old child.

"Ten bulls, sir," said the stallholder. "Ten bulls and it's yours."

"Good." Jim began to take off his coat.

"That's right, sir. Give yourself plenty of room."

Jim folded his coat very carefully. Very tightly. He eyed the target, then placed the folded coat geometrically, and at a slight angle, on the stall's narrow counter.

"I don't think . . ." began the stallholder.

"Son." Jim eyed him, smiling but cold-eyed. "You know—and *I* know—that this shooting-ledge is about three inches too low . . . even for people with duck's disease. Let's say I've sore elbows. I have to rest 'em on something."

The stallholder began to look worried, but in exchange for the coin, handed Jim one of the .22 repeating rifles.

"How many shots in it?" asked Jim.

"Five."

A family was passing; a man, his wife and their tiny daughter. The little girl was neatly dressed, clean-faced and happy. It was their lucky day . . . even though they didn't yet know it.

Jim called, "Your little girl fancy the teddy?"

The family stopped, then drew closer.

"Keep hold of your daddy's hand." Jim grinned at the little girl. "Wish. Wish, as hard as you can."

The man and wife exchanged glances, but didn't move away.

Emily smiled reassurance, and murmured, "It'll make her day."

Jim settled his elbows on the folded coat, nursed the stock of the rifle against his cheek, closed his left eye then gently squeezed the trigger. The .22 made a noise like a gentle whipcrack and a hole appeared slightly above, and to the left of the bull.

"Hard lines, sir," said the stallholder.

Jim lowered the rifle, and said, "Let me see that target."

"What?"

"I have sore elbows. I'm also short-sighted. Let me see that target."

With some reluctance, the stallholder lifted the target from its holder and handed it to Jim.

"A pencil? A pen? Something with a straight edge."

Jim spoke to his wife and Emily opened her handbag and handed him a tiny, gold-plated ballpoint and a postcard.

"What the . . ." A small crowd was gathering, and the stallholder was starting to sweat a little.

"Apart from these targets being smaller than standard, *and* with a bull barely capable of taking a hole made by a two-two." Jim carefully drew a line from the centre of the hole, through the bull, then measured, with great exactitude the distance between the two centres. "Apart from that, old son, this rifle isn't lined-up properly."

"Or you're not the shot you *think* you are," countered the stallholder.

"Or I'm not the shot I think I am," agreed Jim. He placed a dot on the line he'd drawn, then handed the target back to the stallholder. "We'll soon know which. Put it back, old son. And *exactly* as it was before."

The stallholder returned the target to its stand. Jim settled himself and aimed—not at the bull, but at the dot he'd made with the ballpoint—and squeezed the trigger four more times. Nobody could argue. The bull wasn't there any more.

"That's four towards it," said Jim, as he straightened up. "Another five shots . . . eh?"

The stallholder made to hand over another rifle.

"Same gun," said Jim. Then, warningly. "And keep that foresight well in view. Away from that cigarette end. Away from *anything* that might warm it up a little and screw everything to hell."

The old target was returned to Jim. Before it was placed into the holder, the new target was carefully placed beneath the old target and the ballpoint dot transferred.

This time every shot blasted the tiny bull out of existence.

"That's nine," grinned Jim. Then, to the little girl, "Keep wishing as hard as you can, pet."

The final target was subjected to the same rigmarole as the second. The edge of the postcard was used as a straight-edge, to double-check, the dot was placed with the ballpoint and, within seconds the bull had disappeared.

"Give the little lady the teddy bear," said Jim as he unrolled his jacket. "And, whatever four extra bulls win . . . let her mother make the choice."

The stallholder beckoned Jim to the farthest end of the stall then, in a whisper said, "What are you, mate? Bisley champion or summat?"

"Never been to Bisley in my life." Jim shook out the jacket and shrugged it onto his shoulders.

"Just keep away from here, eh? I've a living to make."

"A small lesson." Jim dusted the creases from his jacket. "To keep you on your toes, old son. That's all. People who pass this stall, they aren't *all* suckers." As he turned to leave, and almost as a throw-away remark, he added, "I don't normally shoot holes through pieces of cardboard."

22

Tête-a-Tête

IN and around Lytham Square there are a number of neat little cafes. Few are large enough to merit the description "restaurant" but, no matter, they serve tasty snacks at moderate prices and are immaculately clean. You will find no "Joe's Caff" in that particular area.

Like all such establishments, they have their "busy" periods and their "slack" periods, and one of the latter comes up, daily, immediately after normal lunch time; stomachs are full and the mid-morning or mid-afternoon "bite" is not yet necessary.

Char and Ron were in one of these cafes and, because of the time of day, they were the only customers. They sat at a table by the window, and watched the steady passage of pedestrians and traffic as they sipped coffee, nibbled at chocolate biscuits and talked. It was a strange conversation; the strangest conversation they'd ever had.

It was, at once, intimate but at arm's length; soft-spoken, but with an unusual degree of concern. It held quiet urgency, and yet neither met the other's eyes. They both stared from the window, and spoke as if to themselves. The truth was, they were close—closer than they'd been for years—but neither was prepared to acknowledge that fact. There was a mix of constraint and humiliation which prevented much more than a skirting around subjects neither had then the courage to bring into the open.

Char said, "It's too late, of course. I realise that."

"Too late for what?"

"To say how sorry I am."

"No. It's—it's only too late after the injured party's dead."

"You mean . . ."

"It's not *so* important."

"You mean—y'know—you don't care?"

"Yes, I care. I care a great deal."

"In that case . . ."

"It's been done before." Ron sighed. "Thousands of times. Millions of times."

"Not by me. I swear."

"It's the *reason* that chokes me a little."

"Not—not to hurt you."

"To smash Keith's marriage."

"I—I suppose so," she whispered.

"A foul reason." But there was no real criticism.

She nodded, but remained silent.

Then, very timidly—almost shyly—she said, "Is what Emily said true? I suspected, but I've never really been sure."

"I proposed to her. She wouldn't have me."

"Just like that?"

"More or less."

"It—it must have hurt. At the time, I mean."

"You were never second-best," he said gently.

"I wish I could believe that."

"You can."

"Ron, I . . ."

"I was glad she'd refused . . . when we were first married."

She hesitated, then asked, "And after last night?"

"It happened. You say you *made* it happen."

"That's the truth."

"So-o, it happened."

"Will there be—y'know—a divorce?"

"With Keith as co-respondent?"

"No." The smile was genuinely sad. "Of course you won't. You *couldn't*."

"He saved my life," he said simply.

"That doesn't mean . . ."

"It means I mustn't destroy *his*."

There was a silence. It lasted until the last of the chocolate biscuits had been eaten. Then she took a cigarette from her handbag, lighted it, and it was she who re-opened the stilted conversation.

"Where did we go wrong?"

"You didn't go wrong," he said softly. Sadly.

"Both of us, surely?"

"Look at you." For the first time, he turned his gaze from the window. "Anybody. Who'd take you for a grandmother?"

"It's not important any more."

"To you. To any man, but me."

"Not to you?" There was a hint of pleading in the question.

Very quietly, he said, "I love you, Char."

"I don't deserve . . ."

"You deserve more than I've given you."

"It's not *important* any more," she repeated.

"But important enough for last night." Again there was no criticism.

"I swear. The only reason . . ."

"Probably the *main* reason. But not the *only* reason."

"You—you have worries." She was making excuses for him.

"I have worries," he agreed, and his eyes looked into the far distance.

"Share them," she suggested.

"I can't share them." The sigh was deep and long. "Perhaps I can destroy them. Perhaps tonight."

"*Destroy* them?" She frowned puzzlement.

"I wonder," he mused.

"What?"

"What does Jim do for a living?" The sudden change of subject caught her one-footed. "I've often wondered."

"Insurance, surely?"

"Is it?"

"The hints that have been dropped."

"I've always thought Whitehall. Something like that."

"Government?"

"He's never said. Keith we know sells paste jewellery. They all know our profession . . . house agency, estate valuers. But never *Jim's* profession. He's very chary."

"You don't like him?" It was a question shot with surprise.

"I like Emily."

"Obviously." But there was no accusation. "*Not* like that." The quick, half-smile augmented the truth of the words. "You're the one I love. The only one I've ever *really* loved."

"But you don't like Jim?"

"I saved his life," he said slowly, ruminatively. "Keith and I. Between us, we saved his life. I sometimes wonder . . . *should* we have?"

"You were in the same crew."

"Forty years ago today."

"Still . . ."

"It's a long time. Time for things to change."

"And, people?"

"People change. *I've* changed."

"We've all grown older." She hesitated, then added, "*You've* grown a little staider."

"To put it politely," he smiled.

"All right," she admitted. "I wasn't always the bitch I've grown into."

"Not any more."

"If I can make it."

"You'll try."

He gave her time to finish the cigarette. No hurry. For the first time since he could remember they were at ease with each other. Not *comfortable*—but with luck that would come—but without the underlying tension he'd grown to accept as normality. At that moment, he could have said anything to her—made any admission—and she wouldn't have flown at him. He was sure . . . *almost* sure. But he wanted to be doubly sure. Give it the rest of the day. See how things went. Then he might know what to expect.

He wasn't a praying man, but as he turned to look out of the window once more, something not far from a prayer snagged into his mind and stayed.

Meanwhile, she smoked the cigarette and secretly watched his face. Not a handsome face—he'd never claimed to be handsome, never even claimed to be good-looking—but a kind face. A long-suffering face, with sad, spaniel eyes. The bald dome of his skull. Not funny, not really. Not funny, at all. No toupee. That was Ron. He was bald, so he was bald . . . but no make-believe. No lies. With something of a shock, she realised that her husband was probably the most honest man she'd ever met. The most honest, and one of the saddest.

He waited until she'd squashed the end of the cigarette into the ash-tray, then murmured, "This is the last time, Char."

"Because of last . . ."

"No! Because we aren't what we were."

"If—if that's what you want."

"We were part of a crew," he mused. "A good crew. But that crew broke up forty years ago. It's so *stupid*."

"If you don't want . . ." She hesitated, then said, "We could leave this afternoon. Not bother about tonight."

"No. The car won't be ready. Anyway . . ." He turned, smiled at her, covered one of her hands with his, and said, "They'll expect us. We promised. And tonight could be the most important night of all."

23

Fleetwood

IT lacks the flash of Blackpool. It lacks the toffee-nosed superiority of Lytham St. Annes. It is Fleetwood and, although there are no inclines, it evokes visions of up-the-cobbled-hill-for-a-loaf-of-Hovis. It seems to have a bit of everything, but not enough of anything. It is, of course, a fishing port, masquerading as a holiday resort, and the result is vaguely disappointing.

Whitby can do it. So can Bridlington and Scarborough. Fleetwood *can't* but it would take an expert architect-cum-town-planner to explain why. It has a promenade; a Toytown affair from which waves made dirty by the passing of ships can be seen with little pleasure. It has a theatre; the sort of theatre which bills top "stars" who, in turn, encourage the exclamation, "Good God! I thought he retired years ago." It has a beach; not a large one and often oil-polluted. It has municipal gardens; beautifully kept, but fiddling in size. It has a quay —of course it has a quay—it is a fishing port; but, find it if you can and, having found it, find the way *onto* it.

The impression is that too many people have tried too hard, and none of them have succeeded. Too many "experts" have been pulling in different directions. For a town of its size, somebody has asked too much . . . far too much.

And yet, like a mongrel dog at Crufts, it has its own untidy charm.

Ada liked it.

"We used to take the ferry to Knott End," said Keith.

"What's at Knott End?"

"The ferry, back to Fleetwood."

"But that's silly."

"You do silly things when you're on your holiday. That ferry trip was *very* important."

"Did you ever stay here?"

"Good Lord, no. Blackpool. We usually visited Fleetwood, just the once."

"For the ferry ride?"

"And the tram ride, here and back. On top of the cliffs."

"I'd have stayed here," she said dreamily. "I wouldn't have stayed at Blackpool. I wouldn't even have *visited* Blackpool." Then in a sadder tone, "You're going to find me very boring, aren't you?"

"Not yet," he smiled.

"No . . . but eventually."

He looked at her with narrowed eyes. She was being serious. Or at least, half-serious. It worried and irritated him. He'd tried. All day—every minute, since they'd entered the dining room for breakfast—he'd tried. Little kindnesses. Minor courtesies. He'd gone out of his way to display affection. All that—and with the nagging guilt of the previous night's escapade preying on his mind—and she *still* wasn't sure. *Still* wasn't satisfied.

"We'll find somewhere to eat," he grunted.

"I mean what I say," she said gently. "I'll bore you."

"Hellen didn't bore me." He quickened his pace and headed away from the seafront.

"I'm not Hellen."

"No, thank God!"

"Keith!" The quiet savagery of his remark shocked her.

"Hellen wasn't all she was cracked out to be. Ask that brother of yours when we get back."

"Wally?"

"Dear Wally." The tone was ugly and over-flowing with self-hate and contempt. "I've been hearing things about Hellen—and Wally—and Christ knows how many other 'Wallies'."

"Keith, I want to know what . . ."

"This place looks as good as any."

He grasped her elbow and turned her into a one-of-a-hundred eating places. Not dirty, but not too clean. Not what he might have chosen, but he was in no mood to be fussy. He sat down at the nearest table and, after a slight hesitation, she also lowered herself onto one of the chairs. A waitress arrived. Like the place, the waitress wasn't specifically dirty . . . she merely gave the appearance of not being *quite* clean.

She said, "You're too late for lunch, luv. I'm sorry but . . ."

"You serve food of some sort?" interrupted Keith.

"Well—yes—we could serve beans on toast, but that's about . . ."

"Beans on toast, for two."

"Tea?" The waitress scribbled into her grubby order book.

"For two."

"Right, luv."

The waitress hurried away.

Ada's eyes were glistening, and she was blinking when she spoke.

"Keith, I've a right to know . . ."

"About Wally? Of course you have. About Wally and about Hellen."

"If—if . . ."

"They were humping away like crazy, while I was out flogging cheap rings and brooches. That in a nutshell. And not only Wally."

"Y-you're lying," she whispered.

"Why the hell should I lie? What do I gain by lying? What the hell does that make *me*?"

"I don't believe you."

"Does it matter?" He fumbled a cigarette from its packet, and it wobbled in the flame of the match as he lighted it. He swallowed some smoke down the wrong way and a fit of coughing doubled him up but, even as he was coughing, he rasped, "In Christ's name, what does it matter what *you* believe? What *anybody* believes? The truth's the truth . . . not believing it doesn't make it *un*true."

She took a handkerchief from her handbag, dabbed her eyes, then blew her nose. It was a definite effort, but she steadied herself. Public exhibitionism was something she hated, therefore she steeled herself to take whatever Keith was obviously anxious to throw at her.

In a steady enough voice, she said, "I loved Hellen, Keith. That's no lie. I truly loved her. And I . . . I find it hard to believe that in her condition . . ."

"Before the damned asthma stopped her gallop."

"And you knew this when you married me?"

"The hell I . . ."

He closed his mouth, knowing it was too late. Knowing that the guilt had won, and that all Emily's fine advice had been a monumental waste of time. He smoked the cigarette, jerkily, and waited for the cross-examination he knew was on its way. It came, of course, but much more gentle than he'd expected. Much more gentle than he'd expected. Much more gentle than he deserved.

"You *didn't* know this when you married me?" Her voice was strained, but steady.

"It would have made no difference."

It was a clever answer. It wasn't *meant* to be a clever answer. It wasn't even meant to be evasive. It was merely the truth, but it almost switched the direction of her questions.

"Assuming what you say is true."

"It's true. I have it on very good authority. Two people. Two separate people . . . and not at the same time."

"People who knew her well?"

"Of course. Otherwise—like you—I wouldn't have believed them."

"But not Hellen herself?"

"Would she? Would *any* wife?"

"*I* would," she said simply and the cigarette trembled even more and his eyes widened in amazement. In the same steady voice, she said, "If I was ever tempted. If I was ever . . . weak. I'd tell you. Of course I would. I couldn't live with myself if I didn't. What sort of marriage is built on secrets?"

And, God, he wanted to. How he *wanted* to! It was like pressure building up inside. But it wouldn't come. He opened and closed his mouth twice. Twice . . . almost. *But it wouldn't come*.

Instead, he raised the wavering cigarette to his mouth, then muttered, "It wasn't just the once. Umpteen times. She wouldn't tell me that. Nobody could forgive *that*."

The beans on toast and tea arrived. There was a clatter of knives and forks, a rattle of cheap crockery.

The waitress said, "That all, luv?"

Keith nodded, and the waitress left.

For all of ten minutes they ate in sad and moody silence. It was a miserable meal. A poor meal, in a poor cafe and they were poor company for each other. Shame and strained loyalties made for utter wretchedness. The anger—a man's anger, when he knows he's wrong but hates the contemplation of admitting his wrong—had evaporated. It had been replaced by wildly fluctuating indecision. He truly loved this wife of his. Didn't want to hurt her, but knew he *had* to hurt her, if his yardstick of honesty had to match hers . . . and he *wanted* it to match hers.

He lowered his knife and fork onto his half-eaten meal and, in a quiet, unhappy voice, said, "We have to talk."

"About last night?" She continued eating, but it was merely a means of doing something with her hands; a form of not *quite* concentrating upon his words. A useless shield, with which to ward off something of which she was secretly terrified.

"What about last night?" His voice had a groaning, wounded quality.

"I don't know."

"I mean, why . . ."

"You were in a raging temper." She paused, then added, "That or very unhappy."

"So . . . obvious?"

"Keith." She still held her knife and fork, but rested her wrists against the edge of the table. "Please tell me," she coaxed.

"I—I called in to see Ron and Char."

"Why?"

"After—y'know—the crack Char made at dinner."

"Such a mountain, from such a mole . . ."

"Ron wasn't there."

"And Char told you about Hellen?"

"Yes." He moved his head in a single nod.

"My God! And you *believe* her? You . . ."

"Emily verified it this morning."

"Oh!"

"They can't *both* have been telling lies."

She remained silent and watched his face.

"That's—that's it." Again, he drew back from the edge.

"Not all of it," she contradicted gently.

"How d'you . . ."

"Verification from Emily. It should have made you even more angry."

"Oh!"

"What was it you just said? 'Ron wasn't there'?"

"He . . . wasn't there," he stumbled.

"Just Char?"

"Y-yes."

"Keith . . . *please*."

"She was—she was ready for bed . . ." And then, his mouth dried and he couldn't end the sentence.

"And you finished up in bed with her," she said sadly.

"More or less," he nodded.

"And you've taken it out on *me*."

"I'm sorry," he groaned. "God knows why. God knows how. I didn't *want* to . . ."

"Don't be such a damned fool!"

"Ada, I swear . . ."

"You may be sorry. I credit you with a conscience. But don't say you didn't want to. That's something I *won't* believe."

She lowered her knife and fork onto the plate and, a little unsteadily, stood up.

She said, "Get the bill. Let's get out of here. I need some air."

24

The Arcade

THE youth was of a kind; the only-mugs-work-for-a-living kind. He was a complete nutter, to whom terror was a legitimate coinage, and he dressed and acted the part. He was built big, and aware of the fact. He strutted where lesser mortals walked. His progression was in a straight line; normal people barred his progress at their peril.

From the bright yellow, coxcomb, Mohican hair-style, the single ear-ring with its tear-drop ruby, the open-necked, black leather, zip-up windcheater with its intricate patterns of brass-headed rivets, the skin-tight jeans, held in place with a three-inch wide belt, complete with silver buckle, to the hand-tooled, fancy "cowboy" boots, he looked exactly what he was and what he claimed to be. A hell-raiser. A trouble-maker. A young hooligan who delighted in seeing apprehension in the eyes of all who saw him; who was insulted if he *didn't* see that apprehension.

He was leaning against a pin-table machine, feeding coins into the slot, flipping the steel balls and watching the gaudy lights flash and scatter as the balls bounced from spring-loaded uprights. The pin-table arcade was his haunt. His home-from-home. His "headquarters" from where he emerged to organise some new devilment.

He was surrounded by his buddies. His "clan" as he liked to call them. Each gaudily attired, but none daring to outdo, or even match, the overall outfit of their leader. They, too, looked upon the pin-table arcade as their chosen "headquarters".

It must be understood that it was that sort of an arcade. Crummy to a degree. A real hole-in-the-wall dump, and almost a mile inland from the sea-front. It was used by few people other than the coxcombed youth and his clan and when, more than an hour previously, Jim and Emily Bathurst had walked its length to enter the tiny office at the rear, it had been deserted.

Now, as Jim opened the door and left

the office, he accidentally bumped into the pin-table at which the youth was at play. He put out a hand to steady himself and as his hand rested on the edge of the pin-table, the youth leaned forward and brought his closed fist down, like a hammer onto Jim's knuckles.

"Watch it, you stupid old sod," snarled the youth.

Jim smiled, turned to Emily and murmured, "Obviously, a product of our better public schools."

Emily stood aside, to allow the two strangers to leave the office and enter the arcade.

What followed was something Coxcomb and his pals would never forget. It just wasn't in their book of rules . . . or ever had been.

The clan were watching their leader for some sign which might hint at his next move. They were, therefore, unprepared for the "stupid old sod" elbowing them aside to stand face-to-face and almost touching Coxcomb. Equally, they gawped as the honed edge of a smoothly produced switch-blade caressed the underside of Coxcomb's jaw.

Jim glanced at the hair-do and said, "Let's say Custer's arrived, and this isn't the Battle of Little Big Horn."

There was a movement among the clan; the hint of a surge forward towards their leader. The arcade echoed to the sound of a shot, a hole suddenly appeared in the flooring immediately in front of the would-be rescuers.

One of the strangers held an automatic pistol loosely and easily in one hand.

"To prove it's loaded," he explained coldly. "To prove it works. Proof that it will take a knee-cap off or break an arm, is available, if necessary."

The clan backed off a few yards and watched, fascinated.

Coxcomb wasn't frightened . . . yet.

"What the fu . . ."

"Don't say that word." The blade moved. Coxcomb clapped a hand to his ear as the tear-drop ruby and the lobe of his left ear clattered onto the glass top of the pin-table. "I've read the book, old son. So has my wife. Neither of us approve of the gamekeeper's language."

Again the blade moved. This time to Coxcomb's crotch. Jim bent the youth backwards over the pin-table, holding a fistful of windcheater leather in his left hand. The blood from the lobeless ear dripped and spread on the glass of the pin-table's surface.

"You owe my wife an apology for even *thinking* of using that word in her presence," said Jim.

"What the sodding . . ." Coxcomb closed his mouth as he felt the blade penetrate his skin, through the tight jeans.

"One ball at a time," promised Jim softly. "And don't think I won't. And don't think I can't."

"Who the hell are you?" Fear—something Coxcomb had never before known—flickered at the back of his eyes. The penny was dropping, fast. He'd suddenly entered a league he didn't even know existed. He breathed, "Who the hell *are* you?"

"I," said Jim, calmly, "am the 'stupid old sod' who is about to emasculate you, if you don't say the magic word."

"I'm—I'm sorry." Then as the blade moved a fraction, a shrieked, "I'm sorry! I've said it haven't I? *I'm sorry*!"

"Son," said Jim, cheerfully, "you've just saved your manhood. You're obviously not as daft as you look." He turned his head, and addressed the clan. "You lot. Disappear into the woodwork, where you belong."

"As the man said," added the character with the gun.

The clan scattered out of the entrance to the arcade. The gun was pocketed. The switch-blade disappeared as smoothly, as swiftly, as it had been produced. Coxcomb was left to nurse an incomplete ear with one hand and his crotch with the other.

Jim spoke to the man who'd shot a hole through the floor.

"The idiot who runs this place. Tell him —from me—Hiawatha and his tribe are barred."

"Yes, sir."

"Everything else is under control?"

The two men nodded.

"We need one more in the team, but leave that with me."

"See you next year, sir," said the man with the gun.

"I'll be in touch. Same date. You arrange the rendezvous."

They shook hands all round, then Jim and Emily walked from the arcade.

25

The Zone of Ozone

THAT is what it was once called, and might still be called by aged holiday-makers. The old brochures carried coloured pictures and, always, the caption was "the Zone of Ozone". It lies between Blackpool's North Pier and Bispham. It is the only "quiet" part of Blackpool. Indeed, north of the Derby Baths, it is almost lonely.

Like everything else in Blackpool it is, of course, carefully planned and, in the main, man-made. Nature has been cunningly augmented; the high cliffs, which tower above a magnificent expanse of sand and sea, are criss-crossed with well-kept tarmac paths; the jutting hunks of stone—some as big as a small house—have been artistically positioned, and, be it whispered, quite a few are well-weathered and carefully sculptured monuments of reinforced concrete.

Nevertheless, between the tram-tracks

and the main road at the top of the cliffs, and the promenade which arrows along towards Cleveleys at their base, there is a high-placed green almost as wide as that at Lytham St. Annes, and a good deal longer. More than that. Many people will swear that the breeze which comes from the sea at this point is the best, most instantly remedial air in the world. It comes in by the lungful and immediately revitalises. It carries the whiff of salt, often spiced by the sweet smell of newly mown grass.

Keith and Ada Parkinson sat on the grass and gazed out to sea. Even in their present mood of wretchedness, the peace and the air combined to act as a soothing balm to both hurt and conscience. The occasional rattle of a passing tram seemed muffled and lost under the dome of a wide sky dotted only with a handful of tiny, cotton-wool clouds.

"They used to travel this stretch at not much more than a whisper," remarked Keith. "Now, they're like the rest of the world. Noisy. Knackered."

In front and below them the tide-line was almost out of sight. Acre upon acre of firm, damp sand, spoiled only by two rows of footprints. In parts the sand was in ripples; like corrugated cardboard positioned in tastefully thought-out curves. In other parts the beach was billiard-table smooth with, here and there, shallow hollows in which sea-water caught the sun's light and shredded it as the breeze moved the surface of the water.

"The posh part of Blackpool." He spoke quietly, as if to himself, but he knew she was listening; only *pretending* not to hear. "Lots of modern flats. Must be nice living here. Must be nice to *afford* to live here."

He was wrong, of course. In late autumn and winter the breeze from the west built up into a howling gale. At Illumination Time the tableaus set up along the tops of the cliffs were ripped from firm moorings and flung across the tram-tracks. The salt and fine particles of sand which the wind carried scoured paintwork and (as any resident could have told him) re-painting of exterior woodwork was an annual drain on an already stretched budget.

They'd left Fleetwood, and when they'd reached this stretch of the coastline he'd parked the Cortina and she'd followed him to this very private part of the resort.

She sat with her knees up to her chin and her arms clasped around her shins. Almost a foetal position, and perhaps symbolic of her silent misery. Keith was stretched out, propped up on one elbow. He knew how she felt—*thought* he knew how she felt—and his inconsequential talk was whistling-in-the-dark stuff. He was scared. Deep-down scared. A complete cock-up; his whole life, a complete cock-up. Therefore only the past, his young teenage years, were worth remembering and worth talking about.

He plucked a blade of grass, began to chew it, and said, "Every year. Before the war, every year. A week's holiday at Blackpool. We used to stay down south. Just this side of the Pleasure Beach. Off Waterloo Road. Same place every year. We used to book the rooms a year in advance. As we left one year, we'd book the rooms for next year. A nice place. Homely. Not a hotel, of course. I never thought I'd stay at a place like The Cave. A boarding house. Provide your own food. The landlady cooked it for you. You gave her the breakfast eggs and bacon the night before. You paid for the cruet. I can remember it on the bill at the end of the week. "Use of cruet". . . whatever it was. It was always sunny. Glorious weather. Funny, that. I can't remember it *ever* raining. It must have done, of course. But—like the war, I suppose—you only remember the *good* things.

"Y'know, I've never been to the top of the Tower. All these years. All those visits. Never once to the top of the Tower. I was a bit frightened, I think. Still am, I suppose. It's a hell of a height. They say it sways slightly in a gale. Shouldn't wonder. They say it's *made* to sway—y'know—*expected* to sway. Built to take it, sort of. A foot—twelve inches—in a really high wind. Must be a bit scary, if it's true.

"I remember the wheel. The Big Wheel. Biggest ferris wheel in the world. It went with the Tower. The Tower and the Big Wheel. The two together. Like salt and pepper. Like the cruet we used to have to pay for. I once went on the Big Wheel. About half the height of the Tower, I suppose. About that. But high enough. High enough for me. I remember . . ."

"Shut up!" It was softly spoken and she

continued to stare at the horizon, but the two words had the quality of a scream.

"I'm sorry," he muttered. "But what else? What else *can* I talk about? What else is worth saying?"

"Not the past." She remained rigid. "I don't want to know about the past."

"No. I'm . . ."

"I don't want to know about Blackpool. *Or* Lytham St. Annes. I don't want to see either place again."

"If that's what you want," he said gently.

"If we *have* to talk, let's talk about the future . . . *our* future."

"Do we—do we have one?" he asked timorously.

"That's up to you." She turned her head and looked at his face. In a kinder tone, she said, "It really *is* up to you, Keith."

"No more," he promised, urgently. "I swear—anything—never again."

"I think I believe you."

He almost smiled his relief, and the tears pricked the back of his eyes as he said, "We'll go home. We'll call at the hotel, pick up our things, then be on our . . ."

"No." She shook her head. "Never again. But I don't like running away."

"It won't be . . ."

"I want to face Char knowing she can't hurt me. I want to see her expression when she realises she's played the role of cheap tart for no good reason. I want to watch *her*. I want to hurt *her*."

"Ada." The tightening, hardening of the tone worried him. "You and me. I—I thought . . ."

"It has nothing to do with you and me. That's a thing of the past. You've made a promise and I believe you. You've been weak just the once . . . and it's a poor wife who can't overlook a single weakness in her husband." Her eyes glittered as she added, "But Char's another kettle of fish. She thinks she can get away with things. Anything! Well, not with *me* she can't and that's a lesson she has to learn."

26

Fish and Chips

THE Woolworth's clock showed half-past three, and the crowds were at their thickest. Thousands had already eaten; queueing in passages and on stairways, in the dozens of restaurants, waiting for places at tables to become vacant. Having eaten, they'd returned to the prom and the sands; ant-like in both their numbers and the manner in which they pushed and jostled in their everlasting hurry to cram as much noisy enjoyment as possible into each minute. It was Blackpool at the height of the season, and nowhere on God's earth was quite like it. Nowhere on God's earth was as rowdily happy. Nowhere on God's earth did money change hands as quickly for cheapjack pleasure.

As they pushed their way past the open stall, Emily said, "I thought you said something about oysters."

"That was yesterday." Jim weaved a way

past a group of arm-in-arm youngsters singing and waving Coke cans.

"Those blue points look tasty."

"No. Up here." He guided her from the crowded prom and into a comparatively quiet side street. He smacked his lips, and said, "Fish and chips."

"At The Lobster Pot, of course?"

"Where else?" grinned Jim. As they made their way to the rear of the Tower buildings he discoursed upon the subject. "Why in hell's name can't they fry decent fish and chips south of the Humber or north of the Tees? Why not back home, in London, for God's sake? It's supposed to have *started* there. But you want decent fish and chips in the Smoke, you have to go to some flash eating dump and order it in French. And when it comes it's buggered to blazes by all sorts of additions. Simple fish and chips. There's a knack in it. They have it up north. Down south they haven't a clue. Jellied eels. Who the hell wants jellied eels? Rock salmon. What the hell's rock salmon, when it's at home? Haddock or Cod. King Edward spuds. That's all it needs. So where's the big secret?"

They moved into the single-door

entrance of The Lobster Pot and began to climb the carpeted stairs.

Jim Bathurst knew his onions. He also knew his fish and chips. He knew that pseudo-connoisseurs of that dish insisted, with their dying breath, that Harry Ramsden's, at White Cross, Guiseley—between Leeds and Bradford—was the biggest and best fish and chip emporium in the United Kingdom: which in turn meant the world. He also knew they were wrong on both counts. One of the biggest and *one* of the best—that without doubt—but Hull can boast a "land-and-sea" eating palace three floors high (in effect three Harry Ramsden's one on top of the other), and scattered around the northern counties are a handful of restaurants capable of pipping Harry Ramsden's at the post as far as flavour is concerned. The Lobster Pot at Blackpool is one of them, and Jim Bathurst knew this.

The lunchtime crush had cleared, and he chose a table away from the other eaters and alongside a window from where they could look down onto the heads of the crowds below. They settled into their seats and a cheerful young waiter arrived to take their order.

Jim said, "Haddock and chips for two, lad. With mushy peas. Tea, bread and butter. And we want salt and vinegar. None of your tartar sauce and no lemon juice."

Fifteen minutes later, while their taste-buds wallowed in uncomplicated grub, they talked as they ate. Neither had need to go into specifics; the talk, while incomprehensible to a stranger, needed no amplification as between themselves.

Jim said, "We need an extra man for the September job."

She nodded.

"An extra decoy . . . to be on the safe side."

"You'll find somebody."

"I was thinking about Keith."

"Keith?" She raised slightly surprised eyebrows.

"Keith or Ron," he amplified. "But Ron's anchored to that house agency he's built up. Keith's a free agent. He covers just about the whole country flogging merchandise."

"I suppose so," she agreed.

"As I understand it nobody tells him where. Nobody tells him when."

"As long as he makes sales."

"It's just a matter of reliability."

"He's reliable." This time *her* certainty made *him* raise his eyebrows.

"Last night he bed-hopped with Char," she said calmly. "The last person he'd want to know *that* is Ada."

"Not just rumour?"

"He made me mother-confessor."

"Ah!" Jim's ready grin touched his lips. "Good lass. We have the poor old chap by the goolies."

"Don't hurt him," she said gently.

"Hurt him!" He looked shocked at the very idea. "I love the lad. *You* know that."

27

South Pier

BLACKPOOL South Pier; the shortest, the "baby", of the resort's trio of piers. The impression is that it has not yet grown to adulthood. Unlike the Central Pier and the North Pier, it has no jetty; when the tide is fully out you can lean over the rails at its slightly bulbous end and there below you is firm, wet sand. It forms one arm of an artificial cove, with the convex curve of the open air baths swinging out from the promenade less than a hundred yards from its entrance and, diagonally across the swarming prom, is the main entrance to the Pleasure Beach.

Its pavilion is neither large enough, nor luxurious enough, to merit the top stars of its sister piers and yet, prior to World War II, it annually housed one of the alltime great pierrot shows. *The Arcadian Follies*. ("A change of programme every Thursday and Monday"). The Manx comedian, Harry

Korris—the man who, during the war hosted radio's *Garrison Theatre*—complete with a company of bobbled and frilled concert-party entertainers, gave innocent happiness to audiences without the need of either smut or innuendo.

In some strange way the South Pier has retained this innocence. This refusal to become "with it". This determination to remain a "family" pier. Perhaps the shade of Harry Korris scares off the snide merchants. Or, on the other hand, perhaps the close proximity of the Pleasure Beach helps; hives off the undesirables and draws them into a rowdy, no-holds-barred world in which they feel more at their ease.

For whatever reason, the South Pier remains a very pleasant, unpretentious haven of comparative peace.

Ron and Char Powell sat on deck-chairs within easy distance of the pier end and enjoyed ice-cream cones. It was a perfect measure of their new-found (possibly *re*-found) relationship that they were content to do just that.

They'd taken a bus from Lytham St. Annes to Squires Gate and from there a tram to the South Pier. It was their favourite pier. Unlike Ada they knew this coast; knew Blackpool; knew where the tiny backwaters of tranquillity could be found. In the old days—the *very* old days—they'd often strolled to where they were now sitting and, in deckchairs like the ones they were now sitting in, had snoozed away a sunny afternoon. Half-asleep they'd heard the scream of gulls and the splash of waves against the pier's uprights; holiday noises which went with the warmth of the sun on their upturned faces. In the background—in the *far* background or so it had seemed—the murmured sound from the Pleasure Beach had been some sort of synthetic lullaby. Almost soothing and eye-drooping. Soft noise, warm sun and gentle sea air. There'd been some wonderful holidays, once upon a time, and part of those holidays had been a deck-chair on the South Pier.

Probably they knew it. Probably they were both aware of the simple reason for being there. A reaching back; a wish and a hope that almost amounted to a prayer. That time might somehow reverse itself and turn the once-was into the here-and-now.

Ron reached the last half-inch or so of

his cone. He placed what was left on the ball of a thumb and flicked it high into the air. The breeze caught it and blew it aside, but before it could land on the planks of the pier a gull swooped, mouth wide, and plucked it from its fall.

"They can still do it," he said softly.

"We used to smuggle slices of bread from where we were staying," she reminded him. "Just to do that. Just to watch them."

"And lump sugar for the donkeys."

"Why," she mused, "was it always *lump* sugar on holiday?"

"Why did we always have sarsaparilla? But only when we came *here*?"

"The shop won't be there any more."

"No . . . more's the pity."

"Why so many things?" she sighed. "And why always the *best* things?"

She finished her cone and he took a new handkerchief from his pocket, shook out the folds and handed it to her. She wiped her hands, handed it back and he wiped his hands before stuffing it into his trouser pocket.

"Little things. Important things," she said sadly.

"I know."

"I'm so very sorry," she breathed.

"Not all your fault. Let's settle for fifty-fifty."

Their arms hung loosely by the sides of the deck-chairs, and the deck-chairs were close together. For a moment their fingers touched. A hint of the one-time magic sparked across.

He nibbled his lower lip for a moment, then said, "Char. I love you . . . whatever."

She turned her head and smiled, then said, "The great moments of truth, my dear. Whatever made me think I could ever *not* love *you*?"

To outsiders—to strangers seeing them and taking things at face value—a bald-headed, stoop-shouldered, vacuous-looking man and a mutton-dressed-as-lamb woman trying to look younger than her age. Thus a snap judgement, but snap judgements are notoriously suspect.

28

The Proposition

WHOEVER planned and laid out the gardens of the Cave Hotel might have done so with privacy in mind. The neatly-cropped, two-foot-high hedges bordering the lawns do not interfere with the view from either the dining room or the sun lounge, but at the same time ensure that strollers along the geometrically placed walk-ways can see all around them; can be sure that no unwanted eavesdropper is hiding behind some bush or tree.

A situation of which James Bathurst approved.

Ada and Emily had gone to their respective bedrooms to bedeck themselves for the evening's festivities. Ron and Char had not yet returned to the hotel. Jim had button-holed Keith in the hotel foyer and had suggested a quiet walk in the gardens, prior to their donning dinner-jackets and bow ties. Somewhat puzzled Keith had agreed and now as he smoked a cigarette—as Jim puffed lazily at a cigar—he walked slowly alongside his friend and wondered what all the mild secrecy was about.

"Care to make a bob or two?" opened Jim.

"Er—yeah—I guess," fenced Keith.

"September. Just for one day."

"I'm sorry. I . . ."

"Working for me, old son."

"I suppose," said Keith carefully.

"Just the one day."

"Doing what?"

"We'll come to that later." Jim drew on the cigar. "Round Oxfordshire way."

"I could take a day off."

"Not mentioning it, of course," said Jim hurriedly.

"I'm more or less my own boss."

"Champion." Jim nodded slowly. He added, "It's confidential, of course. I don't have to stress that."

"I—y'know—I didn't know."

"Very confidential," insisted Jim.

"In that case, I won't tell anybody."

"Grand." Again the slow nod, followed by a draw on the cigar. "The actual date

—the actual place—I'll let you know later. In good time though."

"What—er—what exactly do you want me to do?" asked Keith.

"Drive a car."

"Oh!"

"That's all, old son. Drive a car as fast as you can—with safety, of course—at a given place, at a given time."

"Just that?" Keith frowned.

"For which," said Jim deliberately, "you get five thousand."

"Five *thousand*!"

Jim nodded.

"*Pounds?*"

"Used notes. Tax free."

"And—and you call that a bob or two?"

"A figure of speech." Jim grinned. "Right. Are you on?"

"I'd—I'd like to know a little bit more before committing myself."

"Very confidential, of course."

"Of course."

"Well, now," Jim waved the smouldering cigar at waist level as he explained. "You drive this car, see. Not your own car. We'll provide the car. Secondhand, but apart from that all clean and above board. We're not talking about nicked cars. Just a fast car. At the right time you drive the car away from a certain spot. I'll tell you when and where later. You drive fast. Chances are you'll be alone . . . almost *sure* to be alone. The police chase you . . ."

"The police!"

"It's all right, old son. You've done *nothing*. The most they can get you for is speeding. That's important. That's *all* I want them to get you for. Nothing serious. Just give 'em a bit of a run for their money."

"Look, Jim, I . . ."

"It won't be *you*, Keith."

"Eh?"

"Well, it *will* be, of course it will. But a different name and address. A *genuine* name and address. We don't fool around with gimmicks. Driving licence, insurance, certificate of ownership. All genuine . . . when they catch up with you and ask for credentials. And you don't have to worry. They can check till they're blue in the face. Everything straight and above board."

"It sounds like it," said Keith sarcastically.

"Y'know what I mean, old son."

"No." Keith sounded well out of his depth. "I'm damned if I know what you mean. I only know what it *sounds* like."

"What's that?"

"A criminal set-up. Some sort of getaway stunt."

"You won't end up in nick," said Jim solemnly. "You have my word on *that*."

"You keep using the word 'we'," said Keith.

"Uh—huh."

"Who's 'we'?"

"Let's say—what? Whitehall."

"Bullshit," said Keith bluntly.

"You asked."

"I expected a reasonably honest answer."

For six slow paces there was silence.

Then Jim said, "You a Fleming fan?"

"Fleming?"

"Ian Fleming?"

"Oh, you mean James Bond? That sort of thing? I've read most of them. Seen some of the films."

"It's not like that," said Jim gently.

"Y'mean double-zero-seven thing?"

"It doesn't work that way. No government agent has a so-called 'licence to kill'."

"Go on." Keith's voice was a little breathless.

"Good books," said Jim. "Easy reading. Entertaining."

"We're not talking about books, are we?"

"No." Jim paused, then added, "We're talking about real life."

"Okay. Tell me about real life."

"Y'see . . ." Jim chose his words very carefully. "It's a lousy world, Keith. And some people go out of their way to make it even lousier. Anarchists. Trouble-makers. You know the sort of bastard I mean. If all else fails, they have to be—y'know—*removed*."

"Killed," said Keith bluntly.

"Somebody has to do it," said Jim in an oblique answer to the single word remark. "A handful of people take that risk. Whitehall contacts them . . . *they* take the risk."

"You, for example?" said Keith softly.

"*Somebody* has to do it," repeated Jim.

"For Christ's sake!" Keith suddenly exploded. "We're here, in a decent hotel, at a respectable holiday resort, and you're telling me you *murder* for a living. More than that—as I see it—you want to drag *me* into it."

"Five thousand pounds," said Jim softly.

"For committing murder."

"Hell, no." The ready grin curved Jim's lips. "Kennedy was clobbered. All right by the other side, but they're damn near as good as *we* are. How many shots? Come on —tell me—how many shots?"

"Two. I've seen the newsreel umpteen times. One shot . . ."

"Two shots my arse," interrupted Jim, irritably. "Most witnesses swear to three. Some say four. A handful even say five. All from different directions. That was the way it was done, old son. *The professional way*. And—take it from me—Oswald was the patsy. A man like Oswald couldn't organise a vicarage tea-party, much less the assassination of a president. The *real* way—the *only* way—screw up the evidence. Have coppers running in all directions at once. It's a sort of conjuring trick, old son. Keep 'em busy watching the right hand while the left hand's doing the important stuff."

"And that's how you make a living?" breathed Keith.

"I've already said . . . *somebody* has to do it."

"'Somebody' had to kill President Kennedy."

"True." agreed Jim slowly.

"Answer the sixty-four thousand dollar question. Had the price been right, would *you* have assassinated John Kennedy?"

"It would have had to have been one hell of a price."

"But you'd have done it?"

"Let's say, I'd have given it careful consideration . . . at the right price."

"Right." Keith drew deeply on his cigarette. "Check me. Tell me if I have things straight. By profession you're a killer. In less polite language, a murderer. You murder for money. Which, as I read things, means you'll murder *anybody* for money. It's your job. Your profession. Not just Whitehall. Anybody! If the price is right, you're the 'hit man'. Come September you've something lined up. Whoever you're after has some sort of police escort. That's where *I* come in. I hive at least one police car off away from the scene of the action. Innocent little me. While you're committing murder, *I'm* conning the cops." He took a deep breath. "No way, Jim. *No way*."

"Five thousand," murmured Jim.

"Not for five *million*."

"You'll not get that," Jim chuckled, "but I'll tell you what you *will* get if you turn the offer down. A broken marriage."

"Emily can't keep a secret," said Keith sadly.

"Son, Emily and I *have* no secrets."

"Nor," said Keith pointedly, "have Ada and I . . . so the answer still has to be 'No way'."

"Hey, Keith." They stopped their slow walk and Jim rested a friendly hand on Keith's shoulder. "We're buddies. Forty years and more."

"A long time," agreed Keith.

"I've told you things—confidential things—I wouldn't tell any other man alive."

"You have indeed." Keith smiled.

"Just—y'know—I want to live. I want to stay free." He seemed to have difficulty in saying the words. "As you put it I kill for a living. Murder other men for hard cash. I can justify it."

"You wouldn't do it otherwise," agreed Keith.

"I love you Keith. I love you like a brother."

Keith nodded.

Softly, sadly, Jim said, "I don't want to kill to stay alive. To stay free. But I will if necessary. You understand?"

"Perfectly."

"Fine. Fine." Jim patted the shoulder affectionately. "I knew you'd see things my way." The ready grin lit up the face. "We'll have a dinger of an evening, old son. A real dinger. This little talk. It never happened . . . okay?"

29

The Cavern Room

THE Cave Hotel does not cater for "conferences". It has no need to; its prices are such and its clientele so steady that "package deals" are out, and an influx of eager men and women carrying clipboards during the day and cluttering up the bar at night would very soon chase away far too many valued and regular guests. Nevertheless, even in The Cave, there is a room set aside for "functions". Select, top-drawer wedding receptions, for example. (*The management request that the scattering of rice or confetti be as limited as possible*.) The annual—sometimes bi-annual—get-together of sedate (and, of necessity, wealthy) professors and practitioners of some of the less flamboyant sciences. Geology. Astronomy (*never* Astrology). Botany. Egyptology. Thus, this room—this "functional" room—while rarely boasting a waiting list is, nevertheless, used with moderate regularity.

It is called the Cavern Room. It enjoys this title merely because it is part of the Cave Hotel. It in no way *resembles* a cavern; there is no attempt to give it the appearance of a grotto; no imitation stalactites hang from its ceiling, no mock-stalagmites rise from its carpeted floor and to be quite sure nobody has any illusion, green is barred from both its colour scheme and its illumination.

It has an oak-beamed ceiling and waist-high oak-panelled walls. The tables (which can be fitted firmly together to produce a single table of any required length) are of the same dark, seasoned wood, as also is the large, shelved and cupboarded sideboard which takes pride of place along one wall. The ceiling and all other wall-surfaces are painted an ivory colour which in turn sets off the spotlessly white linen and china. Illumination comes from tiny chandeliers and wall-lights whose shades and crystal have a faint orange tinge, thus softening the near black-and-white general decor. It is a very "homely" room; a room in which much genteel and academic pleasure has been enjoyed.

The "do", organised and paid for by Jim Bathurst, was about to start in the Cavern Room.

All three men wore dinner-jackets and black bow-ties. They looked smart; even Keith, whose clothes were hired for the occasion. Jim wore a broad silk cummerbund and a row of miniature medal ribbons on the left breast of his jacket. Emily wore an ankle-length, pale blue evening dress, with an RAF-badge brooch picked out in tiny sapphires on a silver background. Char had black silk trousers and a loose-fitting, long-sleeved, high-collared matching smock; a distinctly "Chinese" look, complete with fire-breathing dragons ornamenting the smock in gold, silver, scarlet and green thread. Ada's dress might best be described as "becoming". Called by the better-class chainstore from which she had bought it as "a party dress", it might equally well have been called, by more snooty establishments, "a cocktail dress". It had a light floral design of autumn tints, it was calf-length, with three-quarter length sleeves and it fitted well.

Externally, then, they made an elegant sextet as they stood in a group, near the window of the Cavern Room, while two waiters put the finishing touches to the table set-out. Meanwhile they sipped apéritifs and chatted. The talk was shallow rather than strained; what had happened since they first arrived at the Cave Hotel was skirted around; the weather, half-humorous political remarks, the various strengths and weaknesses of county cricket teams . . . these were the shaky bricks which went to build a wall of non-conversation. Jim chuckled a great deal and sipped neat whisky. Ron said least of all and toyed with a brandy. Keith, Emily and Char stayed with sherry and remained, outwardly, friendly enough. Ada, surprisingly, had chosen a Bloody Mary; she sipped at it gingerly and joined in the chatter only occasionally, but enough to ensure that she was not excluded from the five who remained from the original half-dozen. Not a group of strangers then. On the other hand not a group of close-knit, life-long friends as previously. Acquaintances? Rather more than that . . . indeed much more than that. But in some strange way without true comradeship. In a phrase, they weren't real buddies any more. Only make-believe buddies; once-upon-a-time friends who yet lacked the courage to acknowledge that their friendship was no longer firm.

The older waiter walked over to Jim, stood by his shoulder and awaited an opportunity to speak.

"Whenever it's convenient, sir."

"Eh? Oh, good. Wine poured for the opening toast."

"Yes, sir."

"Plenty of champagne ready?"

"On ice and waiting, sir. More bottles available, if necessary."

"Champion." Then to the others, "Right, folks. Nosh time. Take your places round the table, please."

It was an oblong table. Place-cards showed where each one of them was expected to sit. Jim sat at the head of the table and Emily at the foot. On Jim's right sat Ada and on her right, Ron. Char sat on Jim's left and, next to her, Keith. Ada watched the others. She guessed that some sort of a ceremony opened the dinner.

On her right Ron whispered, "Get ready

to stand up. We start with the old Flying Mess toast."

Jim stood up. The others also stood up; the men at as near to attention as possible without making themselves look too ridiculous.

"Raise your glasses, ladies and gentlemen." Jim was suddenly a transformed man. Serious to the point of solemnity. He picked up his glass of wine, held it high, and the others followed suit. "A good night, a clear sky and a well-marked target. And here's to the next man to die."

With the exception of Ada, they murmured, "Here's to the next man to die." Then they drained their glasses.

The solemnity dropped from Jim like a cloak, he grinned at them and said, "Right. This is it. Now, eat drink and be merry. The hangar doors stay locked until we've scoffed ourselves stupid . . . then they're open. *Wide* open!"

30

The Hangar Doors

STRANGELY the meal had seemed to renew the old comradeship. The meal and the booze. Jim, Keith and Ron. They were like brothers, with Emily and Char their doting sisters. All the awkwardness had disappeared. All the tiny hatreds and bitternesses weren't there any more.

Ada thought she could appreciate the reason, even though she could not fully understand. These five had lived through a war. They'd seen death—violent, uncompromising death—at first hand; lived with it; cocked a snook at it; even laughed at it. That opening toast. "Here's to the next man to die." God, it had been like raising your glass to Old Man Death himself; at once terrifying and magnificent. And in the old days they'd *meant* it. One of them *would* be the next man to die . . . and soon.

She couldn't remember the war. Not really. Schoolgirls, born and brought up in the countryside, miles from any major town, couldn't be expected to remember a war—even a war of the scale of World War II—as anything other than an inconvenience. There'd been rationing, of course but the odd pig, and even an occasional beast, had been secretly "dropped", and nobody had *really* been hungry. She could remember the Land Army Girls, of course. And the Home Guard, which, out there, had been something to giggle about behind their backs. An occasional villager who'd chosen uniform rather than continuing to work on the land. Now and again, an aeroplane high in the sky and the adults demanding silence while they concentrated upon the nine o'clock news on the radio. Snippets of memory, then, but they all added up to very little. To *nothing* when placed alongside the memories of the other five.

But she supposed (indeed, she was sure) that the men and women who'd fought the war—those who'd been part of the actual *shooting* side of it—must have built up a bond capable of withstanding just about anything. They'd not merely faced death, they'd laughed in its face. Mocked it daily with that macabre toast.

And yet . . .

Why the celebration? Because they'd lived, or in memory of those who had died? Or merely an excuse for the airing of memories? And, if that, what was so wonderful about remembering years of killing and being killed?

Odd, too, that Keith had so rarely talked of those years. Hellen had; at the slightest opportunity she'd told and retold episodes from the past. The glories, the heartbreak and, more than once, the blind stupidities which it seemed had been part of Bomber Command in general and the squadron she and Keith—and Ron and Jim and Char and the others—had been part of. The raids. The waiting. The wounded. The dead. And (perhaps above all) the shattered nerves of those who had gone and come back far too many times. But not much about Keith. Never much about Keith. But . . . if she *had* been cuckolding him. And, on reflection, it wasn't out of the question. She'd been bright. Full of life, even during the asthma period; when the attacks had not been on her, she'd joked and laughed and (with hindsight) *could* have been. And certainly Wally was no angel. Something of a hellrake. The wild man of the village, in fact.

So . . .

But that didn't *quite* answer the question. Why had Keith brushed aside all questions about his flying days in the RAF? In all other things he was a mild extrovert; not objectionably so, but he liked to talk. So *why?*

Meanwhile, she contented herself with table-talk while she enjoyed a remarkable meal. *Hors-d'Oeuvre des Gourmets. Salmon en Croute*. Pheasant in Bordeaux. She declined the *Steak au Poivre*, but was fascinated by the preparation and flaming of it alongside the table. But she could not resist Ice Cream with Liqueur as a dessert. And, of course, the wine. Her glass was never less than half-full; the waiters (the number had doubled to four, not counting those who came and went carrying the hot food from the kitchens and clearing plates, dishes and cutlery) hovered around, emptying bottle after bottle of the stuff. Good wine, too. Like liquid silk with a slow-fuse attached. She felt happy.

Relaxed. And just a little squiffy as the meal drew to its close.

On her left, Jim treated her as he might have treated a grown-up daughter. On her right, Ron seemed to look upon her as a younger sister. There were chuckles and mild teasings about her country upbringing, but not snide or hurtful in any way. They asked about Suffolk—neither had visited the county—and questioned her about Felixstowe and Ipswich, neither of which she'd ever visited.

Ron said, "I imagine Felixstowe to be a little like Blackpool."

"*Nowhere's* like Blackpool," declared Jim.

Ada smiled and said, "In that case I'm glad I haven't been to Felixstowe."

"You don't like Blackpool?" Jim exaggerated his surprise.

"No . . . I'm sorry."

The twist of the small-talk turned to music; not the conversation of musicians, but a friendly argument about likes and dislikes. Expressed opinions countered by smiling mockery.

"Hellen," said Ada, "used to love the big bands."

"Ah!" A dreamy, faraway look entered Jim's gaze. "Goodman. Shaw. Basie. We—the five of us round this table—lived through an era, my dear. You missed it by a whisker. You don't know *what* you missed."

"She had the records," Ada reminded him. "She often played them."

"Remember when we all broke camp to see Miller?" chuckled Ron.

"All six of us," echoed Jim.

"On the way home I . . ." He hesitated, touched his moustache, then said, "I proposed to Char."

With mock-seriousness, Jim said, "I can't imagine anybody proposing to *anybody* on the strength of three badly-played guitars, a drummer who can't hold his bloody sticks properly and some pansy-voiced idiot bawling unadulterated crap into a microphone."

"It's not *all* as bad as that," argued Ada.

"You like it?" Ron sounded a little shocked.

"I like country and western."

"The plink-a-plonk stuff," grinned Jim. "Cowboy hats and singing as if you've a clothes-peg on your nose."

"I also like good music."

"The big bands *always* played good music."

"Classical music. Symphonies. Opera."

"Oh, my God!" Jim's teasing was merciless. "An eighteen-stone soprano, dying of consumption at the top of her voice, with orchestral accompaniment."

The ping-pong of exaggerated opinion was that between friends. Good friends; friends not to be offended and not likely to take offence. That and the food. That and the wine. Thanks to Jim and Ron, she became relaxed. She wasn't the "odd one out" any more. Occasionally she glanced across the table where Keith was enjoying an equally intimate chatter-session with Char and Emily. Sometimes they met each other's eyes and smiled. Even Char nodded and smiled . . . nor did it seem a false smile.

Odd that happiness—at the very least, surface happiness—could build up after the traumas of the last few hours. Apparently no hatred left; not even towards Char. These were good people; people without whom Europe—perhaps even the world—would today be even more evil than it was.

A jackbooted world. A Gestapo-dominated world. A world of extermination camps and calculated genocide. And when set alongside *that* . . .

Jim drained the last of his coffee and caught the eye of the senior waiter.

"You know the score, old son? What comes next?"

"Yes, sir."

The waiter gave a silent snap of his fingers and, like magic, the table was cleared, except for wine and wine glasses. A champagne glass was placed before each of them, the glasses were topped with champagne, then the bottle was returned to its ice-bucket. It, and two similar ice-buckets, each holding its bottle of opened champagne, were wheeled to within easy reach of Jim. Fresh ash-trays were set out. Two huge, oval trays of chocolates and candy were positioned on the white linen, then two filled cigarette-boxes and a box of cigars.

The senior waiter said, "Anything else, sir?"

"That's fine." Jim nodded approval. He glanced over his shoulder. "All the other waiters gone?"

"Yes, sir."

"Good. Drop the latch as you go out. From here on it's *our* party. Very private. No disturbance . . . who the hell he is, what the hell he wants."

"As always, sir."

"As always, old son." Jim smiled. "We remember, y'see. We have *reason* to remember. Very personal memories."

"Yes, sir. I understand, sir."

Ada felt soft-footed spiders running up and down her spine. The atmosphere in the Cavern Room had changed. There was an expectancy. A sombre waiting for a given moment. Like—yes, like Armistice Day—their own self-appointed Armistice Day. And (to her) a little frightening. The others' expressions showed varying degrees of stern-faced acceptance, but acceptance of *what*?

The senior waiter left, the door closed and they heard the latch-lock click into position. There was a silence of almost a full minute, during which time they all looked at Jim. There was a solemnity which almost amounted to sadness and Jim sat motionless through the silence, his head bowed, as if in prayer. Then slowly he looked up, rose to his feet and reached for his glass of champagne.

The others followed his lead.

He raised his glass and said, "To absent friends."

"To absent friends."

"To Tom, Karl, Pete and Mark."

"To Tom, Karl, Pete and Mark."

"To Hellen . . . rest her soul."

"To Hellen."

"To dear old Susie . . . what's left of her."

"To Susie."

At each toast they sipped champagne, and towards the end Jim looked not far from tears. The others sat down, but Jim remained standing. It took him a moment or two to compose himself, then he pulled a handkerchief from his pocket, blew his nose and the old grin lighted up his face.

"Keith," he said, "you're the champagne wallah. Keep the glasses topped up, we've some talk ahead of us." Then, having glanced at the others, his gaze rested on Ada and he continued, "We've a new member. She needs to be told. We *all* need to be reminded. The hangar doors are now wide open."

31

The Prang

HE told it slowly and with carefully stressed detail. The story of one bombing mission; a tiny sliver of long-ago heroism which, at the time, was a near-invisible part of a war which spanned the world. He missed nothing. He started with the briefing, the collecting of the parachutes and the personal flying gear.

"Then a bus to the dispersal point. Seven of us. The old crew. The lucky crew. No swingers. No stand-ins. We were going to make it, there and back, because we *always* made it there and back. Forty-seven times. This was our forty-eighth. And old S-for-Susie was *our* kite.

"That old Lanc—*any* Lanc—but especially Susie." He was speaking directly to Ada. "Climb the steps and into the door and you *knew*. Blindfolded, you'd still have known. That sweet, comforting smell of hydraulic oil. Just that first check, to stow some of the chutes and give her a quick once-over. God, it was like the finest perfume ever made. The old girl's life-blood. With that in her veins, and the Merlins roaring their guts out, and the guns all cocked and ready, she couldn't *not* do it . . ."

He told of Mark, the flight engineer, checking the gauges. Of Keith, the bomb-aimer, crawling into the nose and making sure the Spery bomb-sight was ready and waiting. Of Pete, the wireless operator, dumping his satchel of pre-flight data and testing the radio. Of the two gunners—Karl in the rear turret and Tom in the mid-upper—making sure the Brownings were in good working order. Of Ron, the navigator, carefully positioning his maps and instruments, ready for use.

"No bloody good without Ron. Susie could take us there. Susie could bring us home. But Ron had to show us the way. He *had* to be right, otherwise we were in the schnook. All I did was drive her. All Mark did was keep the fuel moving. All Karl and Tom did was shoo away the fighters. Everything depended on Ron. If *he* did it right, Keith could lay the eggs.

But if Ron ballsed things up, it was all a waste of time.

"Then it was back to the tarmac—back to the grass, maybe—and sweating it out until take-off. The dispersal hut was handy. The ground crew fannied around, swopping dirty stories, chain-smoking fags. Christ! They were more nervous than *we* were. They had cause to be. Susie was *their* sweetheart, too. If *they'd* screwed her up —some little thing—they mightn't see her again. So we horsed around and kept the worry away by playing silly buggers.

"Tom and Mark were RC. The RC padre rolled up in his jeep. Gave 'em absolution." He frowned what looked to be genuine concern. "I hope it did the trick, that's all. For me? Okay, it said C of E on my identity tags, but that didn't mean much. We had a job to do. Bomb the living crap out of men, women and kids. That's what we were there for. That's what we were trained for—what Susie was built for—and I never *did* figure out how absolution could wipe *that* slate clean. After . . . maybe. But not before . . ."

He told of the waiting. The gradual build-up of tension, and the tricks of masking that tension. By this time he was speaking directly at Ada. As if initiating her into some secret sect of which she wished to become a part. Nor did he merely talk. He *re-lived* it. Every moment. Every second. Every emotion.

"It was Happy Valley. The Ruhr. Dortmund." He glanced at his watch. "Round about now we'd be revving up. Cockpit drill finished. Everybody settling in and ready for the signal from the caravan. Round about now . . . forty years ago.

"Don't let 'em kid you, girl. Don't let *anybody* kid you. We were like the rest. Like every damn flyer waiting for that—or any other—take-off. Shitting bricks! Hitting the Ruhr—hitting *any* target in the Ruhr Valley—made being dragged through hell backwards something to laugh at. We'd been there too many times. We *knew*. The bastards would be waiting. They always *were* waiting. Flack and fighters. Okay, Susie could out-fly every fighter in the sky. Karl and Pete could handle Brownings like nobody's business. And—okay—Susie could absorb punishment and still fly. We knew that. She'd flown through flack too many times for us *not* to know. Girl, we'd come home on only two engines a couple of times already. We'd landed with holes you could have put your head through, but we'd landed. We were a lucky crew. That's why we were doing two tours on the trot. We didn't want splitting up. We jelled. We were a team. A *good* team. Funny . . ." Some of the passion left his voice and it took on a musing quality. "We really believed it. Stick with the same crew and we'd make it. We had the edge. We'd worked out the formula. Together we could do it. Split up and we wouldn't make it . . ."

The other four—Keith and Ron, Emily and Char—were listening, as if hearing it for the first time. As if they hadn't lived through it. As if they didn't *know*. This was no alone-I-won-the-war garbage. This was as raw as freshly cut meat. Savagely honest. And maybe that was the reason for these annual gatherings. To *be* honest. To counter the subtle glorification of something which, while being necessary, had also been foul. And certain it was Jim had the gift of telling it.

"Char was there. So was Hellen. So was Jean . . . you've never met Jean, but she was engaged to Pete and *because* she was engaged to Pete we've lost touch. But the three of 'em. WAAF waitresses in the mess. And *they* knew the size of things. What the day held when the battle order was posted, and our crew was listed. Smiling and laughing. But I've come across 'em. Unexpectedly. Having a quiet weep in some corner or another. Especially if they'd had a hint of the target. The Ruhr, see?

"Dammit!" He was suddenly, and for a moment, very angry. "If they'd only told the truth. The Ministry of Information lunatics. The *real* losses. Not the normal 'one of our aircraft is missing' crap. Christ! Ask around. Ask some of the mugs who made those trips up Happy Valley. We *expected* losses of anything up to one-in-three. It was part of the game. That's the way the dice rolled every time. And Dortmund was one of the toughies."

He paused in the story, and in the pause Keith left his chair and topped up the champagne glasses. Char and Keith reached for cigarettes and lighted them. Emily took a chocolate from one of the boxes and popped it into her mouth. Jim's head had dropped a little. He raised it, as if in silent pride, then continued.

"Dortmund, see? Into flack-land. Secretly we were messing ourselves, but it had to be done. And we had to do it. A good crew. A good kite. We'd make it. Sure, we'd make it. We *always* made it. So we worried inside, but made out it was just one more trip.

"Going out, that's just what it was. Just what it *always* was. One more trip. But once we hit the Ruhr! Jesus Jones, those Kraut gunners were trigger happy that night. Flack. A box-barrage of the bloody stuff for miles on end. Flack and search-lights.

"Y'know why they never get it right on a picture screen? Why they *can't*? It can't be mocked-up, girl. It can't be *done*. Not just a few puffs of smoke and a rough ride. The bloody stuff's *lethal*, and it's like flying through a snow storm. Light as day in the cockpit with the damn beams. Susie, bucking and rearing like a frightened horse. And all the other Lancs. You can *see* 'em. Taking as much stick as you are. Going down like birds in a turkey-shoot. They can't mock *that* up. Those who flew through it know. Those who didn't never *will* know.

"You're talking to yourself. I swear. The mike's switched off, so nobody can hear you, but you're talking your way through the bloody stuff. Counting up to a hundred, maybe. Kidding yourself that when you get there, you'll be through it. Maybe you are. Maybe you aren't. If not, you start on your second hundred. Effing and blinding the bastards down below. Hating their bloody guts. Hating their bloody guns. Just hating. Hating the whole sodding issue. The whole bloody bunch of 'em. Hitler, Churchill, Harris. All the flaming lunatics sitting at home on their big, fat arses while you're up there having your balls shot off . . ."

He choked on the memories. Shook his head, as if to rid himself of horrors he wanted to forget but couldn't. He drained his glass at a single gulp, and Keith stood up and re-filled. When he recommenced speaking, much of the passionate hatred had gone. The simple tale—if such a tale ever could be simple—was continued at first in an almost matter-of-fact voice.

"Dortmund was a bad target. We'd been there before. We knew. Knew what to expect. Forty years ago tonight it was as bad as it had ever been. Ron got us there. Smack on ETA. Keith had the bomb-sight lined up, and my job was to keep Susie straight and level for the bombing run. Poor old Susie. It was like rounding the Horn in a cockle. But she tried. She *always* tried. She was one of us. Let me tell you, lass, that kite had a soul. She was one of the crew. She knew her job as well as any of us. The poor bitch really *tried* to fly straight and level. Maybe she couldn't sometimes. But she knew what we needed for that bombing run, and she always tried to deliver the goods. That night—forty years ago—she was wounded. Badly wounded. But she kept as straight as she could, and as level as she could, and Keith delivered the eggs. Then we were away. Through the flack, like a bat out of hell. Making for the far end of the box barrage, before we turned for home . . ."

32

Flying Home

KEITH re-filled the champagne glasses. Then having returned to his seat—and to Ada's surprise—he helped himself to a cigar. Ada and Emily smoked cigarettes and occasionally helped themselves to candy.

Jim had paused in his narrative in order to sip champagne. Also—or so it seemed—to quieten his nerves and his memories.

A civilised place, the Cavern Room. A civilised place, peopled by well-dressed, civilised people. And yet . . .

The passion and the intensity of the story being told had already transported that room away from the Cave Hotel—away from Lytham St. Annes, away and beyond the coastline of the United Kingdom—and, in effect, placed it thousands of feet above a tormented town in the Ruhr Valley. They were *there*. Distance and time had been eliminated. Five of them were high in the shuddering, flack-wracked air, encased in a wounded Lancaster bomber, forty years previously. And strangely—mystically—they'd carried Ada with them. She was with them; and, because this was her first experience of that peculiar terror, she found tiny nerve-ends jerking and trembling. The tale carried a form of horrifying hypnotism; it mustn't stop—it *mustn't* stop unfinished—and yet the possible ending frightened her more than she'd ever been frightened in her life before.

Not three middle-aged men and two middle-aged women. That in fact . . . but *past* facts were now far more important. Three men in the prime of youth—*seven* men in the prime of youth—two women (*three* women, counting the unknown Jean) at their most attractive age. Fighting, killing, dying, worrying and weeping . . . when they should have been enjoying life. God, the waste! The waste of happiness, the waste of youth, the waste of life.

Jim cleared his throat and continued.

"We thought we were clear of that damn box barrage. We *were*. We'd made it again. Susie—poor old Susie—she'd taken some hammer. More hammer than she'd ever taken in her life before. But she was still up there. Still responding to the controls. Sluggishly. As if it pained her to fly. Physically pained her. And why not? She'd some holes in her. One wing. The fuselage. Everywhere . . . or so it seemed. Three engines, that's all. One of her engines had been damn near blown from its moorings, so she'd *that* to carry as extra weight. But she was still flying.

"Keith had climbed up from the bomb-aimer's position. Ron had given a course for home. We'd made it again, see? We were bloody immortal. Through that damn barrage and none of us with so much as a scratch. Susie had taken it all. The lot!" His voice dropped, quietened a little. "Then she took the last one. The one she couldn't quite recover from."

He paused, as if in silent tribute to the memory of a beloved friend.

Almost savagely, he continued, "God only knows where it came from. The searchlights were still around. Not as many, but they were still there. Nothing new. They always *were* there. You flew through the guns—clear of the guns—but the searchlights probed and fannied around, hoping for a spotting. They didn't often get one. They didn't get one this time . . . I'm damn sure they didn't. It was blind bloody luck. Nothing more. It couldn't have been more. But some trigger-happy bastard, down on the deck, let fly and missed by a whisker. It was almost a direct hit. Shrapnel all over the place. Poor old Susie. More holes than a sieve.

"I stopped a lump of shrapnel. Right in the guts. Right there." He touched his middle. "It went in sideways. Must have. The parachute harness—all the gear we had strapped round us—wasn't touched. That's what kept my innards in place. Without that—without that and other things—I wouldn't be standing here today." A twisted grin touched his lips. "Funny thing, girl. You don't feel it. It's a killer, but at first you don't feel it. After a few seconds, okay. It gets warm, then hot, then hotter than hell. As if somebody's stoking a furnace down there. And you want to yell —scream—and tear the thing clear of your body with your bare hands. They tell me —the smart-arse mind doctors—that you can't remember pain. That *nobody* can recall pain. *I* can, girl. And I don't think

I'm unique. Right this minute I can remember—damn near *feel*—that blow-torch burning my guts away. Deep down inside.

"But it gives you time. Those few seconds. Enough time for me to ask the impossible of Susie. Enough time to let her try to *give* the impossible.

"She's like a string-bag, right? More holes in her than a fishing net. Nose down and diving. She's had enough. She's had the living crap kicked out of her and she's had enough. But she's lady enough to respond. Slowly. Shaking like crazy, she responds. I can ease her gently out of the dive. Trim her a little. Pull her into a gentle climbing position . . . and she does what I ask. Now *there's* a high-born lady for you, girl. There's a queen, like no other queen on earth. I slip her into George, the automatic pilot, and she even does *that. She flies herself!*

"Okay, I'm suffering like crazy. I'm going mad with the furnace in my gut. We're a sitting duck for any fighter around, but Karl and Tom are strapped in—like me—and they're ready to give as much as we take. The rest of 'em—Ron, Keith,

Pete, Mark—they're picking themselves up from the floor and counting the bruises. But the old lady's still fighting. Nose up. Losing height. Sure she's losing height—she shouldn't even be *flying*—but she has her snooty, broken little nose in the air, and she's pointing towards home, and she'll either get us there or she'll kill herself trying." A single tear built up at the outer corner of one eye, then slowly rivered its way down the side of his face. He croaked, "It wasn't *her* fault. None of it was her fault. She loved us, Ada. Don't laugh. She was a thing of metal and struts—rivets and dials, anything you like—but she had a soul. And sure as God, she loved every last one of us . . ."

There was a pause in the story, as he produced a handkerchief and blew his nose. He drained his champagne glass, and Keith tip-toed round to collect the second bottle from its ice-bucket and re-fill all round.

The next part of the story was told, as it had been told to him. How the pain in his stomach had knocked him cold. How Ron and Keith, Pete and Mark had gently eased him from the pilot's seat and carried him carefully to the rest bed.

"In every Lanc. A sort of camp bed arrangement alongside the outer skin. If somebody gets clobbered, that's where they're placed. Pending home and an ambulance . . ."

How Keith took over the controls. How, in every operational crew, the navigator and the bomb-aimer had basic flying knowledge for just such an emergency. How Keith nursed and coaxed Susie over enemy territory. No fighters. No more searchlights. No more flack. The slim, thousand-to-one chance that Susie just might carry them home. How they crossed the coast and started on the long slog across the North Sea.

"That's when I came to. Somewhere over the North Sea. Ron was looking after me. Morphine. He'd shoved morphine into me —we carried little tubes of morphine, with a needle attached, and that's what he'd used—and the pain was still there, but bearable. There was a hole in the fuselage, next to the bed, and Ron had rammed his chute into the hole—fastened it into position with intercom wires—to keep the rush of wind away from me. Friends?" He smiled sadly. "*That's* when you know what friends are.

"I still had my gear on. Chute harness . . . the lot. He'd fixed bandaging all round my middle, but on top of the clothes and the harness. To keep my innards in place, see? That much gumption. That much sense. Keith was still at the controls. Tom and Karl were still at their guns. The others? Just waiting. Maybe praying. What the hell else? That's all we had left. That and Susie . . ."

She tried to visualise it. She tried hard; forcing her mind into the darkness of a mortally crippled war plane, staggering above the black and comfortless North Sea in a last, desperate attempt to reach its base. She tried to feel what *they'd* felt. Jim's pain. Keith nursing the Lancaster homewards, mile at a time. The gunners; fingers curled around triggers, staring into the night sky and watching for some fighter capable of delivering the *coup de grâce* with no real effort. And the rest—the other members of the crew—what of them? Terrified and helpless. The carnage behind them. In effect, clinging to a wrecked aeroplane and praying that it might fly for just a few more hours.

"I dunno. Time didn't mean much. Maybe an hour—maybe more, maybe less—after I'd come round, Mark came down the cockpit and broke the news. We couldn't make it. That simple. Too far to go. Not enough fuel. And the old girl was losing height too badly. Two thousand feet. We were down to two thousand feet, and she was still dropping.

"I was still the skipper. I made the decision. Pete to get onto his box of tricks and send out a fix. Then everybody to bale out. I made that decision. God help me, *I* made it. *I* gave the order.

"Two thousand feet, see? The height was needed for the chutes. Much lower and they mightn't open in time."

"To—to leave you behind?" Ada spoke for the first time since Jim had started his story. The question was low-spoken and harsh.

"Why not? I was a goner. It wasn't heroics, lass. Simple arithmetic. One, or all seven. I was still the skipper." He tasted champagne. "It seemed the right thing to do. At the time, it seemed the right thing. It *still* doesn't seem a bad decision." He paused, wiped the back of a hand across his lips and, in a stronger voice, went on. "The gunners left their turrets. Tom and Karl. Mark opened the escape hatch. Keith put Susie back onto automatic pilot. Then they jumped. Mark, then Karl, then Tom, then Pete. In that order. I know it was in that order, because they each came to wish me luck before they went.

"Ron wouldn't leave. I argued with him. My bloody oath! The things I called him, but he wouldn't leave. His chute was buggered—that's what he claimed—he'd used it to block up that hole, so it wouldn't work. It wasn't worth risking. Maybe. Maybe not. I wouldn't know. Just that he wouldn't leave.

"Then Keith. He came back to see me. To wish me luck. Luck! Christ, I thought I'd run out of luck. All the luck I'd ever had. Then he left for the escape hatch, then he came back. He was going to ride her down. Fly her down. Screw the automatic pilot. He was going to take her down to wave-top height, then try to belly-land her . . ."

He was talking about Keith. Her husband. The man who, a few hours before, she'd been ready to leave. And in talking about Keith—*her* Keith—he was also talking about a measure of cold-blooded courage almost beyond belief. A smashed up Lancaster bomber hitting the North Sea . . . in darkness. A sea capable of taking gargantuan structures like oil rigs and overturning them like discarded toys. The expression "dicing with death" touched her mind. Dicing with death, indeed, and with the dice heavily loaded in favour of a particularly nasty end. For the sake of friendship. For the sake of Jim and Ron. Dear God! In time of peace it passed comprehension.

She glanced across the table. Keith was staring with out-of-focus eyes at the table cloth. Remembering things, perhaps. Re-living that moment of his life . . . reason enough and more for him being there.

"That's what he did, too. Carefully. So carefully. No intercom—that had gone for a burton, way back—but Ron wrapped himself round me. On top of me. And, we all waited for the big splash.

"Jesus wept! It was like hitting a wall. Not Keith's fault. Without him at the controls we'd have nose-dived straight under. But he flattened her at the last minute. Touched with the tail first. Then belly-flopped. Still, like hitting a wall. The sea came in through the nose. Through the smashed cockpit. Everywhere! I don't know what happened. Never *did* know. Don't think any of us did. At times like that you just do the right thing . . . or the wrong thing. One way you survive. The other way you don't. Old Susie tried to stay afloat. She knew. She tried to stay afloat long enough . . . and she did.

"Next thing, we're in the dinghy. Don't ask me how. Don't ask me why the damn dinghy still worked. It did, that was enough. Ron and Keith had dragged me clear. Fixed the dinghy. Inflated it. And the three of us inside. Soaked. Frozen stupid. But we were alive. Even with shrapnel the size of a cricket ball inside me. I was there. Alive!"

Ada dragged her gaze from Jim's grim and pensive face. A movement had caught her eye and she glanced to the right. Emily

—dear, sweet, steady-as-a-rock Emily—was touching her eyes with a tiny handkerchief. Such was the mood of the Cavern Room. Even accepting the fact that Jim could tell the story well; that he'd probably told it a thousand times before. Even accepting the undoubted fact that he was a born raconteur. All that, but the basic truth remained. It was an episode of courage and comradeship of a degree impossible other than in the lunacy of war.

Nor was the story quite ended.

"Late afternoon. That's when Ron spotted the Lysander. Stooging along at a few thousand feet. Why the hell it was there? God knows. We never did find out. An ugly aeroplane, the Lysander. Ugly to look at. Not at all like a Lanc. More like a big, awkward insect. But it was ours and Ron—maybe Keith—sent up a couple of flares.

"They'd kept me alive till then. All through what was left of the night. All through the morning. All through most of the afternoon. Damn it, they wouldn't *allow* me to die. They couldn't *do* anything. Y'know, nothing to help. No First Aid. Nothing like that. Just keep the gear in place. Make sure my guts stayed put. Make sure I didn't get any wetter than I was. Make sure I was as warm as possible . . . which meant not quite as cold as I could have been. But they *willed* me to live. I swear! Half-unconscious most of the time, but they wouldn't let me go under.

"Then the Lysander. Then the Air Sea Rescue lads. Then an ambulance and hospital and an emergency operation. Then Emily." He glanced up the table at his wife. "She took over from Keith and Ron. Nursed me back. Gave me something to live for. Eventually became my wife.

"The others—Tom, Karl, Pete, Mark—God only knows. I gave the order to bale out. I was the skipper. I gave the order. I only . . ." He swallowed. "I only hope their chutes didn't open. That it was at least quick. Not hours on end in that bloody sea." He paused again, and the ghost of the ready grin touched his lips. "That's it, then. That's why we have this annual get-together. To remind us that . . . *that's* how it was."

As Jim sat down, Keith spoke for the first time since the start of the story.

In a low, but very deliberate, tone touched with bitterness, he said, "No! That's *not* how it was."

33

The Flaw

THE words were like a knife slicing through flesh. Thus the hush which followed the words could be likened to a silent scream of anguish. All heads turned to look at Keith. Char's fingers flipped against her glass and the champagne spilled onto the table linen. She looked angry and embarrassed at the same time, and began to mop the spilled liquid with her napkin.

"Leave it," growled Jim. "It's not important." Then to Keith, "What you said *is* important?"

"Just that it wasn't that way." Keith's tone was heavy. He almost sighed the words.

"For forty bloody years we've gathered at . . ."

"For forty years we've toasted a half-truth."

"You're a damn liar!" exploded Jim.

"You've sat here at this table, and every time . . ."

"Jim." His tone carried a sad, pleading quality. He shook his head, slowly, and said, "Not you. Not Ron. Not any of you. Each year, you've told the story. Some years better than others. Never better than tonight. And I've listened and said nothing. Maybe because of Hellen. Because Hellen wanted to hear it that way. Because *she* believed. But Hellen isn't with us any more . . . so the truth can be told, at last."

"The truth? Are you accusing me of . . ."

"You've had your say, Jim." This time Emily interrupted. "We've listened. We believe you . . . *I* still believe you. But Keith has doubts. He's entitled to express those doubts. I don't think he's called you a liar, but . . ."

"The hell he hasn't! He's . . ."

"No. Not a liar." Keith reached for a cigarette. "Mistaken. No more than that. But it's a mistake that has to be rectified."

"Let him speak, Jim," said Emily. "He saved your life. He deserves to be heard."

Slowly—almost with reluctance—Jim nodded. He said nothing. Instead, he lifted the bottle from its ice-bucket, topped up his glass, then passed the bottle round the table. Char righted her glass and re-filled it. Keith lighted the cigarette and when he started to speak it was as if he (like Jim) was only concerned that Ada might learn and understand.

"Since we arrived last night. Such a lot. A whole lifetime. A whole reversal of beliefs and yardsticks. Things of which I'm ashamed, but for which I've been forgiven." He glanced at Char, and they both understood, perfectly. "I should be hated, but I'm not. That demands a price, and I intend to pay that price. No half-truths. No lies. Honesty, above all things. The truth . . . as *I* know it."

He drew on the cigarette, then continued, "What I did that night forty years ago. I was given a gong. The DFM. I don't wear it. You, Jim, you wear your medals. The ribbons. Miniature ribbons as now. Laudable, I *mean* that. They were earned. The DFC. God knows, you earned *that*. But not me. Mine was a con. I know . . ." He waved Jim's interruption aside before it could be made. "Forty years ago tonight. That's what you think. What you all think. What Hellen thought. But it's not true. I *didn't* earn it. What you put in the recommendation . . . nothing like the truth.

"Pete, Mark, Karl, Tom. They'd all gone, remember? You'd given the order. To jump for it. I—er—I didn't. I disobeyed that order, because I was scared out of my wits. *I daren't jump*."

He paused to sip his champagne, to draw on the cigarette, then to clear his throat before continuing, "I'd seen the target, Jim. Dortmund. I'd seen the flack, and all the other Lancs purling down as the flack took them. I'd sprawled there on my belly, in the nose of old Susie, and watched it coming up at us. Watched it coming up at *me*. Anybody of our age—anybody who was a bomb-aimer over a well-defended target—will tell you the same. That stuff's coming up at *you*. Personally. Not at the aeroplane. Not at bomber force. *You* . . . that's all.

"All right. You swallow your guts a dozen times. It's what you're trained to do. But that doesn't alter things. You're still scared witless. And when you crawl up out of that nose, you're like a jelly. I was. Every time.

"Then with Susie shot to pieces. God, I was scared. And we couldn't make it home, and you had a flack wound like nobody's business, and down there was the North Sea . . . *and I couldn't swim*. Still can't. I stood at that escape hatch, and I couldn't make myself jump. I tried. I cursed myself for the coward I was, but I still couldn't force myself to jump.

"So I came back and flew her down. Nothing brave, Jim. Nothing heroic. I earned a medal for being a coward, and I've lived with that knowledge for forty years. Not for your sake. Not for Ron's, or Emily's, or Char's. For Hellen's sake. I've kept quiet about the truth for *her* sake . . . and now it doesn't matter."

He drew on the cigarette, and when he continued, although the words seemed heavy with gall, there was no bitterness in the tone. Just matter-of-factness. A hint of relief almost. As if he'd rid himself of a burden he'd grown weary of carrying.

"That's me, I'm afraid. Keith Parkinson. As false as the trinkets he flogs at cheap shops. Jewels that only *look* like jewels. Something of a make-believe man, eh?" He smiled and added, "That proposition earlier this evening. Knowing what you now know, would you have made it?" He looked directly at Jim as he spoke, then added, "Try Ron. He'll refuse, but try him."

Jim's eye narrowed dangerously.

Ron said, "What proposition's that?"

"Nothing." The words came from the back of Jim's throat. "Nothing of importance."

Emily was at Keith's side. She beat Ada only by inches. She had an arm around his shoulders, and she kissed him lightly on the forehead. They spoke together.

Emily said, "You saved his life. Reasons aren't important."

Ada said, "It doesn't matter, darling. It doesn't matter any more."

Char touched Ada's arm. Gently. Timidly.

Ada looked down and Char breathed, "He saved Ron's life, too."

The two women looked at each other for a moment, then Ada smiled and moved her head in a single nod which was so small as to be barely noticeable and Char leaned sideways and touched Keith's cheek with her lips. From across the table Ron watched and smiled slowly. A strange smile, full of sadness and gratitude.

At the head of the table Jim glowered and compressed his lips.

Emily and Ada returned to their seats. Keith cleared his throat, then took a handkerchief from his pocket and blew his nose.

He squashed out the cigarette, looked to his right, at Jim and said "Well?"

"The right thing for the wrong reasons," growled Jim softly.

"I don't have to live with it any more."

"Oh, yes." Jim's tone held no sympathy. "For the rest of your life, old son. *They* might forgive you. *I* might even forgive you. But what about *you?*"

"I'll try."

"You won't succeed. A bloody coward. One of *my* crew."

"Jim!" Emily sounded genuinely shocked.

"What else? He disobeyed orders . . . because he was scared."

"Karl and Mark. Pete and Tom," said Keith gently. "They obeyed orders. What if *they'd* have been cowards?"

"They weren't." The answer was short and uncompromising. "They were trained, fighting men."

"They're now long-*dead* fighting men," said Char coldly. "Forty years dead. And as I read this how-I-won-the-war-daddy story you tell us every year, you're the man who sent them to their deaths . . ."

"Who the hell . . ."

"If—like Keith—they'd mentally told you to get stuffed, they might even be here, with us. Listening to your annual blather."

" . . . asked you to shove your finger in the pie? You always were a stroppy little tart. God only knows what Ron ever . . ."

"That's far enough, Jim!" Ron's voice had a tone-colour none of them had heard before. Not loud, but loud enough. Not threatening, but carrying a distinct warning. Not argumentative, but with the gloves off, and ready, if necessary. He said,

"It seems we've reached 'confession time'. So be it. Now it's *my* turn. And—fair warning, Jim—you're not going to like what you hear."

34

Guilt

THEY were no longer the close-knit group they'd been at the start of the meal. Nor were they the attentive audience listening to Jim's account of a night forty years before. Not that they were strangers or even estranged. Rather were they friends who suddenly—very suddenly—had found fissures in their friendship. The reason was obvious. Forty-year friendships demand more than an annual meeting to survive; mere comradeship—even the comradeship of war—is not enough. A man is not the same this year as he was last; not the same this year as he will be next. And close friendship is an on-going, perpetual thing. Long interruptions weaken it; deprive it of the food of gradual change.

Thus they were still friends, but not *quite* the friends they'd been a few hours before.

"A thing you didn't mention," began

Ron in a calm, measured tone. "That night in Susie. All the nights in Susie. You and I were officers, flight lieutenants. The others were sergeants and flight sergeants. Keith, there, was a flight sergeant. We—we two —ranked each other. In effect, I outranked you. I'd held a commission two months longer than you had. It means nothing now, of course. It didn't mean much then. We were a crew. We were friends. And in the air *you* were skipper. *You* gave the orders. But after you'd been wounded, what then?

"It can be argued that, when the pilot of a bomber is as badly wounded as you were, there is an automatic relinquishing of command. That he's in no condition to reach sensible conclusions. In no condition to make valid decisions."

"It was my belly . . . not my head," said Jim angrily.

"You couldn't even *fly* her," countered Ron.

"That doesn't mean . . ."

"It means the pain was such, you couldn't think straight. You passed out. Remember. You weren't the skipper any more."

"And you *were*?" There was open contempt in the words.

"Yes." Ron nodded. "The others looked to me. Ask Keith. You were on the bed. You weren't even at the controls. Somebody had to take over." He sipped from his glass then said, "Had I countered your order, they wouldn't have jumped. Tom, Karl, Pete, Mark. They might still be alive . . . that's what I'm getting at."

Jim almost snarled, "You're giving yourself some fine airs and graces, aren't you. Skipper? You couldn't . . ."

"Dammit!" exploded Ron. "I'm trying to lift some of the guilt from your shoulders. Can't you even see *that*?"

"Who the hell says I'm guilty of anything?"

"*I do*." The others stared their surprise at Ron. The quiet, wouldn't-hurt-a-fly Ron. He was flush-faced and genuinely angry. "This pathetic annual charade. What else but a form of penance?"

"Hey. You two . . ." began Keith.

"What else?" Ron wouldn't be stopped. "Jim-the-Lad. Flight Lieutenant Bathurst, the man capable of drinking the whole of the mess under the table. My God! He's little more than a boozed-up lout, when all the tinsel's been torn away. He could fly a Lanc. Big deal! So could thousands of other men. He's had the gall to call *you* a coward. Dammit, Keith, you saved his life. You saved both our lives. If he hadn't given the wrong order—if he hadn't told the others to bale-out—you might have saved *all* our lives. That's the part he can't swallow. That's what chokes him. And now—because it's been explained that all the guilt isn't his, that *I'm* as much to blame as he is—he can't stand *that* either." Ron's voice quietened a little. A weary smile brushed his lips as he said, "The all-or-nowt man. On ops you were the same. We had luck. My God, we *needed* luck with you at the controls. But the one decision that was wrong, and the one decision you can't reverse, Jim. They're still dead. By this time the fish have picked their bones clean. And however hard you try, you can't buy absolution."

Jim muttered, "Bloody parlour psychology." But it wasn't the same Jim, and they all knew Ron had placed his arrow of accusation plumb in the centre of the gold.

"No." Ron was back to his old self-effacing manner of speaking. "I'm sorry, Jim. *I've* lived through it, too. Those four men—young men in the prime of their lives—our friends . . . they needn't have jumped. You could have stopped them. Equally, *I* could have stopped them. That knowledge almost wrecked my marriage. That secret I've shared with you all this time.

"Who knows? Perhaps we needed forty years to screw up courage enough to admit it. Perhaps we needed one of us to die—Hellen—to finally drive the nail home. But this I *do* know. No more get-togethers. This is the last one for Char and me. It's been a bad time. Things . . ." He paused then went on, "Things have happened. Things I want to forget. Last night. Sitting alone on the prom all night. Looking out to sea. Don't laugh. Please don't laugh . . . any of you. But—y'know—I had the impression that I heard them. All four of them. Pete and Karl and Tom and Mark. Talking to me inside my brain. I *heard* them. As plainly as if they were all four standing there in front of me. We're forgiven, Jim. They forgave us as they died. They don't *want* us to be haunted by that order and the fact that it wasn't countermanded. They don't *want* this."

He ended and slowly lowered his head a little as if in silent prayer.

Emily was weeping quietly. Char chewed at her lower lip in order to keep *her* tears at bay. Keith looked ashen, and the cigarette trembled slightly each time he raised it to his lips.

Ada? How does anybody feel when surrounded on all sides by guilt? And that was it. An accumulation of guilt which over the past forty years had destroyed with the slow certainty of cancer. It was an instinctive knowledge on her part because, for the life of her, she couldn't appreciate the "Why?". Nobody had actually *killed* anybody. Nobody had deliberately taken the life of a friend. Why, then, the guilt? Should they all have lived or all have died? Seven of them—the whole crew of Susie—died together with all the dash and glory with which they'd lived together?

Come to that, *was* it dash and glory? Not the way Jim had told it. The way he'd told it—looking behind the actual words he'd used—it had amounted to mass courage which, with a flick of the same coin, could also be viewed as mass lunacy. Whatever else, not cowardice . . . despite Keith's telling of the true reason for their survival.

Ada was well out of her depth and had the wit to know it. She also had the good sense to say nothing.

Suddenly Jim pushed himself upright. The chair teetered then righted itself. A little unsteadily he walked to the door, turned the knob of the latch-lock, then left the Cavern Room. The others thought he'd gone to the toilet. Emily's weeping quietened. Keith finished the cigarette and squashed it out in an ash-tray. Ron rubbed his palms down each cheek, as if bringing back circulation after a spell in biting weather. Those were the only movements made, and nobody spoke.

There seemed to be a mutual understanding that the thing was not finished. That the battle—and it *was*, in its own way, a battle—had not been fought to its final conclusion. Jim was still the unknown factor. Once upon a time, he'd been recognised as one of the death-or-glory boys. The big man. The man who couldn't be quietened and wouldn't be licked.

Well, he was entitled to *his* turn, therefore they waited.

He returned with an unopened bottle of whisky in one hand and three glasses in the other. He re-latched the door, placed a glass in front of Keith and a second glass in front of Ron. He returned to the head of the table, placed his glass on the cloth in front of him and spoke as he unscrewed the top from the whisky bottle.

"Right, you sanctimonious bastards. Right!" He topped his glass with neat whisky, then handed the bottle to Ada to pass on to Ron. "The women can drink what's left of the champagne. The men are on Highland holy water. And before you all drop from your chairs, gassed out of your puny little minds, *I've* a few things to say. *I've* a few fancy little theories to air."

35

The Creed

ADA was no tippler, but even she knew the grape-and-grain warning. A deadly combination. Good champagne followed by equally good, neat whisky. The object of the exercise was to get drunk . . . obviously. They were, perhaps, part-way there already, but this giant on her left was determined to go the whole hog. Stupefication was his aim, and he wasn't going to be satisfied until Keith and Ron were both stupefied.

And yet, strangely, she found herself understanding him. Pitying him. In effect, he was feeding them his own anaesthetic; showing them how *he'd* handled his conscience all these years. Which in turn meant he *had* a conscience . . . which in turn meant he, too, was riddled with this ridiculous guilt.

Meanwhile . . .

"Keith knows." Jim tipped a mouthful

of whisky down his throat, then started quietly enough. "Keith knows, because I told him, earlier this evening. I asked for his assistance and he refused it, but in asking I had to tell him things. He guessed the rest.

"That's okay. He can't do a thing about it. None of you can. Me? I'm Flight Lieutenant James Bathurst. It says so in the hotel register. When I sign the cheque, that's what I'll sign . . . and the cheque won't bounce. Driving licence. Bank card. Register of car ownership. The lot! James Bathurst . . . Flight Lieutenant.

"But try looking that up in a telephone directory. Any telephone directory. Try finding it on an electoral roll. Just try. But don't try too hard. Not unless you want MI5 or Special Branch camping in your front garden. Believe that, you little innocents. Believe it, if you believe damn-all else. Flight Lieutenant Bathurst. Jim Bathurst. He took flight a long time ago. Disappeared up his own anus. So—be warned—don't start looking for him when you leave this hotel."

The glass travelled to and from his mouth and he continued, "All right. That understood, let's go back forty-odd years. Callow youth, eh? Hitler, the Nazi boys, the Blackshirts. What the steaming hell did we know about 'em? What? We were more interested in Oxford bags and plus-fours at that age. Let me jog your memories. A belief. That if Germany and Great Britain pooled their fighting capability, and the Yanks financed it all, there'd be peace forever more. We could police the world. We could belt blue bricks and steamrollers out of any other nation stepping out of line. A legacy from the First World War. Let the enemies become friends, and between 'em they'd be unbeatable. We believed *that*, too.

"What we didn't expect was National Socialism. A dictatorship. A leader prepared to treat international agreements like so much toilet paper. It had to be stopped, and we were the lads to stop it. Maybe that's why we joined . . . on the other hand maybe not. Maybe we joined because every other silly bugger was trying uniform on for size. The reasons aren't too important. Seven of us put RAF uniform on, and we met at OTC. From there we moved on to Lanc Finishing School, and from there to an operational squadron.

"We were part of the war. The *fighting* war. Who the hell cared who we bombed—what we bombed—as long as we arrived back at base for a fried egg? Bloody stupid! Putting your lives on the line for a fried egg and the comfort of sheets to sleep between.

"Then gradually we grew up. Manhood, the hard way. After D-Day—when the khaki jobs moved forward and saw what the bastards had *really* done—we grew up. Fast! I reckon we began to hate. We saw photographs of evil. Cold-blooded, calculated evil. The camps. Slave labour. Attempted genocide. By Christ *I* remember the day the penny dropped. The day I swore I'd kill every sod capable of even *thinking* along those lines."

"The Avenging Angel," murmured Keith.

"Parkinson!" Jim snapped out the name. He emptied his glass and reached for the whisky bottle. Once more he was "the skipper"; forty years had been shed and he was the man in control. As he topped up his glass he said, "You've had your say, lad. You started this hare from its set, remember? All that yellow-bellied crap about why you didn't jump. Nobody interrupted you. Nobody interrupted Powell. Now it's *my* turn."

Ada blinked her astonishment at the change. Gone was the paternal façade, and in its place was the voice of absolute authority. This man—this Jim they'd all near-hero-worshipped—was a dangerous animal. More than that even. He was a dangerous animal, trapped and ready to fight his way to freedom.

He drank whisky and continued, "Use your imaginations . . . if you have any. Without Hitler. Without Himmler. Without Stalin. You can name 'em by the dozen. Here in this country. In America. All over the world. Megalomaniacs with *real* power. Leaders. Top military men. Religious fanatics. They come in all shapes. They come in all sizes. And every right-thinking man *knows*. Shift *them* and a hundred-thousand decent people can go about their ordinary lives. Why the hell should *they* live in order that little people might be tortured to death? And who the hell is there around to hold them in check?

"You may not have noticed. No, you

won't have noticed. You've been too busy hawking houses and fairground tat." He gulped whisky. "But where are all the giants these days? Where are all the men big enough to stop these bastards in their tracks? Ogres, oh yes. Far too many ogres. But no giants. History. It's full of ogres. Evil bastards who've made their own history. From Nero to Judas. From Robespierre to Capone. Ogres who made their own history. Who carved it out of living flesh, and built a fortune on the side. But very few giants to slap 'em down before they grew *too* big . . ."

She remembered stories she had been told—books she'd read—of the great speakers. The reformers with golden tongues. The fearless men who controlled crowds and mobilised armies. Henry at Agincourt. Lloyd George on a Welsh hillside. John Wesley in a pulpit. Such men could turn other men's minds; swerve them from life-long beliefs. The power of words, spoken with a natural skill which amounted to near-genius. This man had that power. Every argument was a proclamation, admitting of no counter-argument.

"We sleep in our beds in this country.

Without fear. Without the possibility that something we've said—some little remark we've made, some thoughtless thing we might have done—might be magnified to form the basis for imprisonment. For deliberately inflicted pain. For banishment to some vault, some God-forsaken spot beyond reach of the rest of mankind. For death even. Speedy death, if you're lucky.

"That, my little fairy-floss innocents, is what democracy is all about. It's what Mark and Tom and Pete and Karl died for. It's what *we'd* have died for. What we *should* have died for, and what we were *prepared* to die for. For forty years we've lived on loaned time. We shouldn't *be* here. But, by God, in that forty years *I've* made bloody sure the other four didn't die in vain."

More whisky. As if to keep the passion flaming inside him stoked up to a white heat. He was away and flying solo. Guns blazing and every other machine in the sky his enemy. He was magnificent, but quite mad.

"I've killed. Sure, I've killed. I was taught to kill. We all were. Trained killers . . . all seven of us. We killed in order to preserve a way of life. Those we were up against tried to kill us—tried to destroy our way of life—but we won. Hitler and his court committed suicide in a Berlin bunker. The rest of the bastards either scattered or took on new identities. But that wasn't the end. Some people thought it was—still think it was—but it wasn't the end by a long way.

"Democracy! It's a beautiful thing. But it has to be paid for. Twenty-four hours a day, every day of every week . . . forever. Too many people want to smash it. Too many people can't live with it and become what they *want* to become. But they can be spotted, and they can be dealt with before they become a real menace."

"Killed," said Keith softly.

"*Executed*."

"For Christ's sake! *Killed*," exploded Keith. "The public hangman 'executed' people. He wouldn't deny he'd *killed* them."

"And they were tried and found guilty," added Ron. "Tell me. Who tries and finds *your* victims guilty?"

"I wouldn't call 'em 'victims'."

"All right. Call them any name you like. Who decides?"

"I'm given orders."

"You're also paid, presumably."

"Powell, you obviously don't approve of what I do for a living . . ."

"To put it very mildly."

". . . but without me—people like me —*you* wouldn't live the life of ease you've grown used to. Neither you nor that wife of yours."

"Bathurst." The newly-found Ron came over in the tone. "'That wife'—as you call her—has a name. Oblige me by using it."

"Oh, by God, yes." Jim's mouth curled into a sneer. "She has a name, all right. She *deserves* the name . . ."

"It's not 'Hit Man'," snapped Char. "It's not 'Mechanic' or 'Blow-away Artist' or 'Ice Man' . . . or any of the other damn-fool terms murderers hide behind."

Keith said, "Jim—in God's name—you *don't*. Surely to God, you don't. All this . . . you're only joking? It's—it's an off-beat joke. A drunken gag of some sort."

"It isn't, y'know." Ron answered the implied question. Sadly, quietly he continued, "We'd a good crew. A better crew never flew a Lanc." He began to speak directly at Jim. "You were a good skipper.

Reckless, but you could handle a Lanc. I agree with you. For the last forty years we've lived on borrowed time. And much of it due to your capability in the air. But you were a braggart then, and you're still a braggart. I'm sorry, Jim. I never liked braggarts. I didn't then. I don't now. More than that, even . . ." The quick smile hinted at sadness and sympathy. "You're the only man I ever met who *enjoyed* the war. Who was openly and obviously sorry to see it end. I've wondered why . . . now I know. *You liked killing people*. Presumably, you still do. This—this thing you do, whatever it is—is a continuation of the war. For you the war didn't end. It never will. You take 'orders', you either can't or won't say who gives you those 'orders'. I don't think you care. Just that you can kill. That's enough. That you, Jim Bathurst, can hold the right of life or death over a fellow-man. That you can still play your old game of cowboys-and-Indians . . . with real bullets."

"This, too, holds real bullets." Emily spoke for the first time. The tiny handgun she'd taken from her handbag was held steady, with her forefinger curled around the trigger. She looked down the table at her husband, and tears rolled down her face, smudging the carefully applied make-up, as she said, "You're on trial, darling. Pray to God you have the right answers, otherwise . . ."

36

Trial

JAMES BATHURST knew the gun. He knew most things about handguns. They were the tools of his trade. He'd bought his wife the tiny, Colt Junior, .25 semi-automatic pistol. He'd had the .22 short conversion unit fitted in order that it might hold a more standard bore of ammunition. He knew it held six shots, each of which could wound or shatter bone; that to be truly lethal the .22 bullets had to be accurately placed in the brain or in the heart; that although it was termed "Junior" —in the hands of a non-expert it was little more than a toy capable of frightening off would-be-attackers—in the hands of a skilled marksman it *was* a deadly weapon. It was less than four-and-a-half inches long and weighed little more than twelve ounces. Such a silly-looking little gun. The immediate impression was that it might be a fancy cigarette lighter. But it was no cigarette lighter. Nor, in the hands of Emily Bathurst, was it in any way "silly".

"What the hell . . ." he began.

"Jim, you've had your say."

"Meaning?"

"Originally ten of us." The tears crept down her cheeks unheeded. Her voice had a slight catch, but other than that was as steady as the tiny pistol. "The crew, Hellen, Char and myself. Now . . . only five. Half of us gone."

"Give it time." His tone was uncompromising. His eyes hard and without even a hint of fear. "Then we'll all have gone."

"Don't!" She moved the tiny pistol a fraction of an inch as he reached for the whisky bottle. "You've drunk enough. I want you as sober as possible. I want you to fully understand."

"Understand what?"

"What I'm going to say to you."

"Understand?" The chuckle was devoid of any mirth. "I understand all right. I understand that you're a gullible old woman who's been influenced by all the hearts-and-flowers crap these two lunatics have spouted. *That* I understand. And if you think . . ."

His hand closed around the whisky bottle. The pistol made a noise like the clap of two palms together. The bottle shattered below his fingers and the golden liquid gushed onto the linen of the table.

Slowly, he opened his hand and allowed the fragments of glass to fall into the golden pool, and for the first time a hint of worry —not fear—glinted in his narrowed eyes.

Ada's hand flew to her mouth as if to block a tiny scream. Char moved her head left, right, then left again—like a Wimbledon spectator—as she tried to watch Jim and Emily at the same time. Ron and Keith glanced at each other, and Ron gave a tiny shake of the head.

It was doubtful whether the sound of the pistol shot had carried beyond the confines of the Cavern Room but, even if it had, it would not have been recognised for what it was. A slight rowdyism, perhaps. Something accidentally dropped. But what of it? This customer Bathurst was able to pay for, and *would* pay for, any damage which might have been caused. The size of the handgun, plus the privacy of the room, plus the high regard in which James Bathurst was held at the Cave Hotel made just about anything possible.

With the possible exception of Ada, they all knew this and the knowledge frightened Ron, Char and Keith. Anything *could* happen, anything at all. And they could do little to stop it while Emily had the Colt pistol and was prepared to use it with such accuracy.

"Emily . . ." began Ron.

But Emily silenced him with a slight raise of her free hand.

"Sit down, Jim," she said, and they realised she was no longer weeping.

Or was she? It was possible to weep inwardly. Ron, of all people, knew this. To freeze the face into an expressionless mask. To tighten tiny muscles until they ached with the strain, but by so doing refuse external signs of heartbreak to show. Too many times—far too many times—he'd performed the trick himself. Emily could do it. Possibly—even probably—she *was* doing it.

Emily repeated, "Sit down, Jim. Sober and seated, that's how I require you."

Jim glanced down at the still-open hand

HNM18

which had held the whisky bottle. Slowly he shook his head.

"No bloody woman," he growled, "is ever going to . . ."

"Sit down, for God's sake!" Keith snarled the outburst. All pretence at politeness was thrown aside. "These last twenty-four hours, I've had a gutful. From you. From everybody." He picked up an empty champagne bottle by its neck and began to hoist himself upright. "Sit down, you big-headed bastard, or I'll knock you down."

"Keith!" Ada was shocked at the explosion of rage.

"The louse kills for a living. You *get* that? He kills for a living. And he had the gall to try conning me into . . ."

Emily said, "Put down the bottle, Keith."

"Look, I'm not going to . . ."

"*Put down that bottle*."

The tiny pistol moved and, reluctantly, Keith unwrapped his fingers from the glass neck of the champagne bottle and relaxed into his seat. And during the small exchange Jim had seated himself. As if of his own free will. As if, during the minor distraction, *he'd* decided he'd rather sit than stand. He watched Emily and waited. They all waited.

"Ron, will you please light me a cigarette," she said gently.

Ron lighted a cigarette. It shook a little as he held it in the flame. She took it in her free hand and raised it to her lips. As she took the first deep inhalation it was quite steady.

She spoke to Ada.

"Ada, my dear, can we trust you?"

"Of—of course." Ada was startled at the question.

"Specifically, can *I* trust you?"

"Yes . . . of course."

She drew on the cigarette, then said, "What happens now is between we five. I mean no disrespect, but it has to do with *us*. Meanwhile, I'd like you to run a little errand."

Ada waited.

Emily said, "What's happened inside this room . . . it *hasn't* happened. You understand?"

"I—I think so."

"You tell nobody. I want your word on that."

"Of —of course."

"Your word. Your solemn promise."

"My solemn promise," said Ada softly.

"Thank you." She took a tiny rectangle of pasteboard from the open handbag in front of her and handed it to the younger woman. "A dry cleaning firm. Remember the telephone number, please."

Ada read the words and numbers on the card, then nodded.

"You can remember that number?"

"Yes."

Emily held out the hand holding the cigarette, and Ada returned the card.

"*Remember* it. Don't jot it down."

Ada nodded her understanding.

As she returned the card to her handbag, Emily said, "What I'd like you to do is this. Go to your room. Put on a coat and find a telephone kiosk. There's one near the Post Office in the square. Make sure you have change before you leave. Dial that number. Allow it to ring three times, then replace the receiver. Count to ten, slowly, then dial the number again. Whoever answers will tell you it's the wrong number, when you mention the dry cleaning firm. Ignore that. Tell whoever answers that you have a parcel for them to collect, immediately. From this hotel. Give them a description of your dress, your age, the colour of your hair. Something they can recognise you by. Tell them you'll be in the hall lounge. Come back to the hotel and wait in the hall lounge. You'll be contacted. Tell whoever contacts you—it'll be a man, at least one man—that *I'll* contact *him*, then go back to your room, pack your bags and wait for Keith. Do you understand all that?"

"Y-yes." Ada nodded.

Keith said, "Look, I don't see what Ada has to . . ."

"She'll be quite safe," Emily assured him. Then to Ada, "On your way out tell the head waiter we are not to be disturbed. That nobody—*nobody*—will be welcome in this room without the personal say-so of either Mr. Bathurst or myself."

Again Ada nodded, rose and walked from the Cavern Room. The latch-lock snapped into position as she closed the door.

"Now what?" asked Char.

"Now . . ." Emily smiled. "Now it's *my* turn. But this time it's a trial. It *has* to be.

You three? Let's call you the jury. Jim, there, he's the accused."

"And you?" asked Ron.

"The judge. The prosecuting counsel. Possibly, even the executioner."

"Some bloody trial," rasped Jim.

"Would anybody care to act as defence counsel?" She looked at Ron, Keith and Char, in turn. None of them spoke. None of them made any sign. She smiled at her husband, "You don't *need* a defence counsel, my dear. You could always defend yourself —justify everything you did—you haven't suddenly lost the knack." She drew on the cigarette, kept the tiny Colt aimed directly down the table, then said, "In legal jargon, then, the opening speech."

37

Accusation

"WE go back forty years. More than forty years. And I can do without *this*." She squashed the cigarette into an ash-tray. "If I deny Jim the solace of whisky, I can do without nicotine . . ."

"Don't let *me* . . ."

". . . to root out the truths of our life together." She refused him the right to interrupt. She quite simply continued speaking; ignoring what was obviously going to be a contemptuous remark. "You—Char—you and Hellen, you knew these men. These flyers. These young heroes who twice, three times a week, invaded enemy air space and dropped bombs on German targets. You knew them better than I did. You worked with them. Alongside them. In the mess and, when they had parties, you were part of those parties. You saw them when they were happy. And what if the happiness was forced? What if much of it was bravado? It was a *form* of happiness, therefore you knew the real thing was at least possible.

"Me? I was a nursing sister. A couple of years older, therefore given to a slightly more serious outlook. More important, I saw them, in the main, when they were broken and miserable. Often without limbs. Often without a cat's chance of ever again living a normal life. The truth is, not many 'Baders' walked through the war on artificial limbs. Most of them either wept or were embittered. That was the 'air crew' *I* saw. A different breed. Shattered giants, many of whom refused comfort."

She smiled at Char as she continued, "Earlier today, I did you a grave injustice. I told you—pretended to remind you—that you caught Ron on the rebound. That he married you because he couldn't marry me. Actually, it was the other way round. Oh yes, he proposed—we'd met at a dance away from the aerodrome—and I wouldn't say "Yes". Nor, come to that, would I say "No". I hesitated . . . and I lost. I hadn't the sense to realise that those young men hadn't the *time* to laze around playing sweethearts and swains. *They* knew. They knew the value of snatched happiness, and that it *had* to be snatched, before it was too late.

"But you see, my dear, all I'd seen was the wreckage. And it frightened me. I didn't want *that* or even the possibility of it. I think I loved Ron . . . it's too far away now to be sure. But *if* I loved him, that's in the past and we're both too old—too world-weary—to allow it to affect our friendship. The fact is, I daren't marry him and didn't, you dared and did. I was the loser. It was I who married on the rebound. I married Jim . . ."

Keith marvelled that the voice was so even-paced and steady. As smooth and unhurried as a moving staircase. A catalogue of facts, simply told and without emotion . . . and yet not zombie-like. As if, over the years, she'd carefully sorted and filed for this moment. Checked and re-checked. As if, had she been asked, she could have taken any incident—any thought or decision—and placed it with absolute accuracy in its appointed slot.

Only the .22 pistol raised the story from that of raconteur.

Only the .22 pistol!

"I knew you—all of you—I met you all, through Ron. To know one was to know the whole crew. I don't have to remind you of that. And to know a crew was to know their girl-friends. Their wives. Ada wouldn't understand that, of course. Only *our* generation. Only the flyers. Only the bomber crews. I think we're privileged people. Privileged, in that bombing had never been part of any previous war and won't be part of any future war. Bombing *that* way. A sort of 'going over the top' each time they went on a raid. Seven of them. Always the same seven. And because it *was* the same seven, each raid tightened the bond of comradeship. I think there'd never been such friendship before—such genuine, masculine love between seven men who before the war hadn't even known each other—and I don't think it can ever happen again. It needs a peculiar circumstance and, without that circumstance, it can't happen. We lived through a war. Through a unique bondage. Through a part of history which wasn't *all* bad.

"I knew Jim, then, through Ron. Through the rest of you. Knew that he was a man's man. He could make decisions as easily as he could snap his fingers. I knew that, too. That he was unlike me . . . I never *could* make fast decisions. I admired him for that, too. He was a giant . . . a giant among giants. A little noisy, perhaps, but afraid of nothing. Nothing!

"Then, when they brought him in with that stomach wound. God, you have to be a nurse—you have to be part of the medical profession—to realise. He shouldn't have been *living*. There's a point where medicine—surgery—stops and miracles take over. Ask any doctor. Ask any surgeon. They perform the impossible, sometimes, but they *don't*. All they do is their best, and they know their best isn't good enough. Something is added. Something they have nothing to do with. A person who should have died, lives . . . and they know *they* haven't saved his life. I think that's why so many doctors—so many nurses—are genuinely religious. They *know* there's something extra over which they have no control.

"That's what happened with Jim. I know. I was on duty. I was there when they undressed him. Cut the harness away. *I* held his stomach—his intestines—in position, until the others could bind him up, prior to rushing him to the theatre. With my own hands, I did the work of stomach muscles which had been torn to shreds. *And most of the time he was conscious*. Grinning up at me. God only knows what pain he was suffering, but he could still smile at a slightly panic-stricken nurse. He could even give a cheeky little wink . . ."

Char reached for a cigarette and lighted it. She'd heard the story before. Vague outlines of it. So had the others. But never in such detail. Never told so quietly, so calmly and yet with such intensity. As if she was doing far more than *remembering*. Re-living, perhaps. Pleading, perhaps. Dragging small but important facts from the depths of her mind in order to be quite certain.

But certain of what?

"I went with him to the theatre. On the operating table. The surgeon. He was a fine surgeon. I'd watched him at work many times. Truly, a minor genius with the scalpel. I can remember what he said, when he saw the wound. When we'd cleaned the area and tied off all the arteries. When we could see, for the first time, the extent of the damage. The exact words, almost whispered through the mask. "I'm not God". But that's what I wanted him to be. God. To mend something which seemed well beyond repair. To make it whole. To *be* God.

"The operation took three hours. A little more than three hours. It was—it was like filling a crater in a road. When we'd removed what was ruined beyond all hope. A crater. An empty space we had to fill. I remember the sweat. The number of times I had to wipe the sweat from his forehead. Surgery . . . forty years ago. You have to remember that. No 'open-heart' stuff. No transplants. That surgeon didn't operate. He *improvised*. What he did wasn't to be found in any of the text-books of the day. He cut and stitched and pulled together. He virtually made it up as he went along . . ."

Ron looked pale and weary as he listened. In the last twenty-four hours he'd taken an emotional battering. And now this. The woman who might have been his wife—the woman he loved second only to his wife—was pleading for something. Pleading, but unaware that her every word was part of that plea. Pleading for a reason. For a valid counter-argument. For something even *she* couldn't fully understand.

So useless. Such a waste of time and heartbreak. Such a waste of a lifetime. Such a waste of *lives*. Tom's life. Karl's life. Pete's life. Mark's life. Theirs and tens of thousands of other lives . . . all wasted. That was the size of her plea. That they all counted for nothing.

And yet he willed her to win.

"After the operation. Again I can remember the words of that surgeon. His disgust at his own inability to perform what he thought was an impossibility. 'Like wall-papering cracks in a falling house. Take him to one of the private wards. At least let the poor bastard die in comfort'.

"But he didn't die. *I'd* decided upon that. A young nurse with only limited experience, but I'd decided. This was one wrecked body they wouldn't bury. He was *my* patient. I missed meals, I did without sleep, I worked all the way through off-duty periods. That wasn't important. The important thing—the *only* thing—was that he'd recover. Fully recover and be a complete man again. It was slow work. Hard work. Never-ending work. At one time it seemed to be touch-and-go . . . which of us would die first. Jim from his wound, or me from worry and loss of sleep. But we made it. Both of us. We made it and, in our own way, we fell in love. A kind of love. *Our* kind of love. When he was up and about—while he was still a little unsteady—he asked me to marry him and I agreed. What else? What was the point of almost killing myself to keep him alive, then allowing him to leave my life?

"You two—you, Ron, you, Keith—had been taken off operational duty and were instructors. Remember? Susie was in the North Sea somewhere. The crew was finished. And when he'd fully recovered, Jim was sent on a crash course and became de-briefing officer at another squadron. De-briefing officer. Why not? He knew as much as any man when it came to interpreting fighter movement, the switch of major defences from one area to another. He knew what the flyers *should* see. What they *should* encounter. The probable losses over various targets. The tricks the enemy used to deflect Main Force from its objective. He'd been a top-rank bomber pilot. He became a top-rank de-briefing officer. Which, of course, meant he was attached to RAF Intelligence . . ."

On the face of things, Jim had dozed off. He was relaxed in his chair, he'd allowed his chin to drop onto his chest and his eyes were closed. His attitude—the slump of his body—suggested bored arrogance. What did he care for a gun trained on him from a distance of only a few feet? A piffling little gun like the .22 Colt pistol? He'd dodged anti-aircraft shells in his time. He'd weaved a way through cannon-fire from German fighters. Every trick. Every ruse. Every trap. He knew them all, and could avoid them all.

He knew the telephone number Ada had been told to dial. Knew what would happen. Knew what this scatterbrained wife of his had in mind. But . . . so what? *His* kind didn't grow on trees. He was valuable. Priceless. Without *him*—a handful of his kind—civilisation would have gone up in smoke years back. The mad buggers would be on the rampage. The Glory

Brigade would have inherited the earth.

Well, that's what some of 'em *had* done —inherited the earth—six foot of the stuff!

"Even then—after we'd been scattered —we still made a point of gathering on this date. Remember? Not like now. Not a five-star-plus establishment. An evening of drinking. A mild booze-up in the back room of a pub somewhere. But we always made it because the bond was far too strong ever to be broken. That's what we thought. That's what we believed. The six of us, toasting those who couldn't be there.

"Then, after the war, it's not a big step from service intelligence to civil intelligence. He had the knack. He could interview, interrogate. MI5—UK security—had a place for him. A sort of superpoliceman. Interviewing doubtful security risks.

"It was a strange time. This thing—this Positive Vetting, as they call it—went on for weeks. Jim. First of all Jim. Then, while he was on the training course, me. Positive Vetting. They'd like to know everything you did, everywhere you went, everybody you spoke to, every day of your life. Virtually! That's what they try for. They never get it, of course. It's an impossibility. But they try. They ask thousands of questions, and the answers are all verified. They make you write out a complete biography of yourself, from as far back as you can remember. Everything. Which newspapers you've favoured. Which clubs you've joined. Who you know . . . *everybody* you know. Favourite politicians. Favourite film stars. Favourite radio programmes. *Everything*. Then they try to catch you out in lies. As far as they're concerned mistakes—a slip of memory—boils down to a deliberate lie. It goes on and on and on. And by the time they're satisfied, you're wrung dry. There's nothing—no tiny secret—they haven't winkled out of you . . ."

Jim kept his eyes closed, but listened. He wondered how far this stupid bitch of a wife of his was prepared to go. The whole hog, by the sound of things. Trust a woman! Trust a bloody woman not to know when to stop. Not to keep her damn mouth shut. Jesus, Joseph and Mary . . . didn't she *know?* This stuff was like boiling pitch. They'd both end up as tar-babies and spend the rest of their lives wondering what the hell was waiting round the next corner. Dammit, he wasn't the only one. There were others. And the boys at the top weren't there to take chances.

So shut up, you crazy old cow. You've said too much already. Any more, and there isn't an insurance company in the world would take our money. You want to commit suicide? You want to kill *me*? Fine, go ahead, but not this way.

"Y'see . . ." She almost smiled. "Mr. Le Carré—all the other writers—they never dwell upon the wife. But the wife knows, too. She *has* to. You can't have a husband traipsing off for days on end and not let the wife know. She's *part* of it. That's why *she* has to suffer this Positive Vetting thing. In case—y'know—he talks in his sleep. Some do, I'm told. In case he cracks under the pressure. Then she knows *why*, and can let the right people know. The right doctors, and so forth. Not just some radical quack who might learn things he shouldn't be told . . ."

"Things he shouldn't be told." Keith

frowned his anxiety as the sentence reminded him of where Ada had been told to go, and what she'd been told to do. All this wheels within wheels, and wheels within *those* wheels. The so-called "Hidden Administration". The "departments" everybody knew about, but *didn't* know about. And now Ada knew. She knew a telephone number and very soon—if not already—she'd know a man or men. Not by name, of course, but by sight. She'd be able to describe them.

He'd read a lot. Hawking paste jewellery all over the place had meant staying at hole-in-the-corner hotels most of his life, and he'd developed the habit of going to bed early and reading until his eyes were tired. Biographies. Reportage-style writing. Exposes. Usually paperbacks picked up as he'd travelled and arrived at some town to display his wares. And, okay much of it was imaginative garbage. But even if ninety-five per cent of it was imaginative garbage, that still left five per cent of truth. The misty, mysterious world of espionage and counter-espionage. A very *dangerous* world, and Ada had been sent out to touch the fringes of that world.

He said, "Ada. I don't think you should have . . ."

"She's quite safe." Emily didn't seem to mind the interruption. She smiled and said, "Keith, already *you* know more than *she* does. And there's more to come."

"In that case . . ."

"I wouldn't harm you, Keith. I wouldn't harm any of you, but it's necessary."

"I—I don't see . . ."

"You will."

Ron said, "Have patience, Keith. I have the feeling that this little lot has been festering for a long time."

Keith continued to look worried, but remained silent.

Emily said, "You know Jim. You all know Jim. Enthusiasm personified. Nothing impossible. Never wrong. Never beaten." She paused, as if to gather her thoughts, then went on, "There was this man. Devonport Dockyards. Nothing too serious . . ."

"Classified information." Jim spoke after a long silence. He eyed Emily coldly and growled, "'Nothing too serious'. Talk sense, woman. When MI5 gets interested it's serious. Bloody serious."

"He had to be interviewed," continued Emily calmly. "Jim got the job, but couldn't break him . . ."

"So I broke his traitorous neck."

38

Peephole

IT was to have been such a happy reunion. As every year for the last forty years. Happy, a little noisy, a little boozey. The pattern should have been the same. The hangar doors to have been opened at a determined time, and thereafter a remembering and a glorious wallowing in the once-upon-a-time.

It was what had brought Ron and Char, and Keith and Ada. It was also what had brought Jim and Emily.

But now this . . .

Men kill for a thousand and one reasons. Greed, jealousy, anger, fear . . . even for kicks. Jim had killed for reasons of patriotism; the un-named traitor had refused to admit his treachery, and because of his obstinacy Jim had done what he'd thought was the right thing. The only thing left.

"He was as guilty as hell, but clever

enough not to give us enough evidence to hand him over to the police."

True—quite possibly true—but having made that admission a pin-prick was made in the curtain which blankets off that world-within-a-world, hinted at but never acknowledged. Ron, Keith and Char were shocked at the revelations which followed that admission.

The murder was "sat upon" and for a few days it was touch-and-go. Jim, too, could have died of a "broken neck"; the hanging-shed was still used in those days. His lords and masters in Curzon Street and Whitehall carefully weighed the pros against the cons. They didn't give a damn about James Bathurst personally. He'd killed a suspect. He *shouldn't* have killed that suspect. Outward respectability was of some importance.

But . . .

He'd killed a man and that, of itself, took guts. Many men *feel* like committing murder but (fortunately) few can bring themselves to perform that act other than in hot blood . . . and then they regret it. Bathurst didn't regret it. Nor had it been a hot-blooded killing. When interviewed

Bathurst had even shown surprise at their concern.

"He was a traitor, clever enough to get away with it. If he'd lived, he'd have sold more secrets."

A cold-blooded killing for patriotic reasons. And by an educated man who'd passed Positive Vetting with flying colours. It was something unusual. Something almost unique.

The dead man was quietly disposed of and Jim was removed from MI5. He became a member of one of those fringe groups about which the ordinary man-in-the-street knows nothing; one of those groups which are "attached" to MI5, MI6 or even Special Branch when things grow too hot for any of the officially recognised departments to handle. In the terminology of the group he became a "plumber".

"Plumbing!"

High-powered rifles, handguns, knives, explosives, piano-wire, poison, timing devices. These were the tools of his new trade, and he was taught the expert use of those tools.

"You're a government *killer*!" gasped Keith.

"I dispose of people."

"You *kill* the poor buggers."

"Keith." Jim smiled sadly at his one-time crew-member. "You dropped bombs, remember. You aimed them, then you pressed the tit."

"God Almighty! We bombed *targets*."

"Towns? Cities?"

"Of course. We didn't . . ."

"Peopled by men, women and kids. For Christ's sake, man. How many do you think *you* killed?"

"For heaven's sake, Jim, we were at war."

"We're *still* at war."

The argument raged. Voices were not raised, first names came back in use and, on the face of things, it was all very civilised, but the passion was there nevertheless. Some of the tension seemed to ease; Emily still held the tiny pistol ready, but its presence was almost ignored and she raised no objection when Jim lighted a cigar.

Ron backed Keith; the '39–'45 years were "special".

"We weren't murderers. We were *airmen*."

"Try explaining that to the people of Dresden . . . even today."

"We were given orders. We obeyed them."

"*I'm* given orders. *I* obey them."

"But damn it all, Jim, *we're not at war*."

"You poor, purblind innocents." Jim shook his head in mock sorrow. "We're *always* at war. There's no 'declaration', that's all. Other than that we change enemies as often as we change our underclothes."

"Classified Information". The term need never have been coined. Char listened, but said little. She had this intuitive feeling that Jim was arguing—almost fighting—for his life. He argued with Keith, he argued with Ron, but the gist of each argument seemed to be directed towards Emily, and Emily listened and seemed to weigh each argument against each counter-argument with infinite care. As if, inside her head, there was apothecary scales and she was silently watching each pan as it slowly rose and fell.

There was a lull in the argument, as if each side was waiting for an expected second wind.

Very gently, very distinctly, Emily said, "And the others?"

"What others?" Jim's hand jerked a little and the ash fell from the cigar and splattered onto the table-cloth.

"Those you weren't 'ordered' to kill? The side-line killings? The ones you were *paid* to murder?"

It was as if she'd been waiting for him to exhaust all his excuses, before coming in with the clincher.

She took up the story where she'd left off, and nobody interrupted her.

"The 'plumbers'. That I can understand, I think. The argument has some validity. If by killing one man you ensure the peace of the realm, that killing *can* be justified. If by killing one man you remove the leakage of highly secret information to a potential enemy that, too, I can understand. These so-called 'spies'. They're grubby little people. I don't mean *physically* dirty—although some of them are that, too—but they have grubby little minds. Greedy little minds. They're no great loss to the human race. They rarely have strong emotional ties . . . by the nature of things, I suppose. If all else fails, therefore, I can see a need for official 'plumbers'.

"But, you see, these official murderers —these 'plumbers'—are part of the Establishment. By stretching things a little I suppose you might call them a form of 'civil servant'. And civil servants aren't well paid. The pay is adequate, but it doesn't run to this. To a private room at a hotel like *The Cave*. Which means there are temptations.

"I'm told that the first murder is the most difficult. That after the first it becomes progressively easier. The conscience becomes more and more impermeable. No more doubts. No more bad dreams. Not even the acceptance that what you're doing does *not* bear reasonable comparison with the work of a slaughterman in an abattoir. The expression 'killer'. It takes on a new and terrible meaning. And wicked men—men who make it their business to learn these things —come to know you. Come to list you as a man capable of taking human life without a second thought. These men—they're known in the underworld parlance as 'brokers' —approach you and tempt you and the temptation is very great.

"Such names." She smiled, sadly. "Such mock phraseology. 'Plumbers'. 'Brokers'. 'Hit men'. I rather think every 'plumber' is a 'hit man' on the side. Why not? So goes the argument. The professional is always the best, and the best has to be paid for. Officialdom doesn't seem to mind. It keeps the 'plumbers' in practice, I suppose. It certainly augments their official salary . . . over-shadows it, in fact. A 'plumber' lives in style. Nothing but the best. But only because he's also a top-class 'hit man'. Tax-free, too. It makes places like the Cave Hotel possible. Luxury living. *Real* luxury. But it has to be paid for. And it has to be lived with. The knowledge. The disgust. And—and there comes a breaking point."

"You mad bitch."

Jim grunted the insult as he raised the cigar to his mouth. His fingers seemed to tremble and, before his lips could close around the cigar it dropped onto the carpet alongside the chair. He stooped to retrieve it and, when he straightened in the chair, the switch-blade was open and on his lap, hidden from view by the folds of the tablecloth.

He drew on the cigar and said, "Mad and hypocritical. Tell them you haven't enjoyed the luxury."

"I've accepted it," she admitted softly.

"How—how many?" Keith seemed to recover his breath, before he asked the question.

"In more than thirty years?" Emily moved a shoulder.

"I exterminate vermin." Jim had recovered his composure. He waved the cigar airily. "I do what the law can't do. What a lot of people would like to do, but daren't."

"Brave man," mocked Emily.

"Tell me." Char's voice was level and steady as she asked the question. "Would *we* be 'vermin' if the price was right?"

"I can answer that." Keith spoke. "The right price, he'd have assassinated Kennedy. He made that admission to me. Earlier, when he tried to proposition me."

"So, who *are* the 'vermin'?" asked Char.

"People other people wish to step over." Jim chuckled, quietly. "Think about it, my little innocents. Any of *you*—*all* of you—

have learned things in the past few hours. You didn't ask. You didn't *want*. Blame a stupid old woman who's gone soft in her old age."

"No!" Emily's eyes hardened. "Blame a woman who's lived with evil too long. Who's listened to that evil call brave men cowards . . . but that was too much."

"What—what do we do?" breathed Ron.

"We vote."

"Vote?"

"Whether or not I squeeze this trigger. It's been a trial, Ron. Haven't you realised that? Forty years ago we saved his life. You, Keith, a forgotten surgeon and myself. The question. Has it been *worth* saving?"

"Who are we to . . ."

"The hell it has," snapped Keith. "If he's what he claims to be. If he's done what he claims to have done . . ."

"He has. Believe me. That and more."

"Christ!" whispered Ron.

Jim drew on the cigar, blew smoke, then said, "She's asking for backing. Justification. A vote of bloody confidence. Should she shoot me? Shouldn't she shoot me? A show of hands, please. All those in favour of instant retribution, please show."

"That makes us accessories," said Char.

"No." Emily shook her head.

"I don't see how we can't be . . ."

"By this time," said Jim, "Ada will have company."

"Look . . ." began Keith.

"A very smooth organisation." Emily's voice carried sad memories. "The 'plumbers' sometimes don't function properly. They die. There's never a corpse. Never a killing. What's left of them . . . vanishes. They never *were*."

"Vote, you yellow-livered bastards," snarled Jim. "Put her out of her misery. You'll be safe. So, vote and be damned."

Slowly, Keith raised a hand. Char hesitated then she, too, lifted a hand. Ron shook his head, slowly.

"A hung jury," mocked Jim. He dropped his hand below the line of the table. "I'm not raising *my* hand, so where do we go from here."

"I have the casting vote," said Emily flatly.

She squeezed the trigger as he launched himself along the table, the flick-blade out front and ready for use. The .22 slug went in along the side of his neck, but did nothing to stop his momentum. She jerked herself upright and squeezed the trigger three more times as the blade reached out for her body; three tiny bullets grouped at chest-centre.

Blood trickled from Jim's mouth as he gasped, "You stupid—stupid—stupid . . ."

Then he was dead, and the hand holding the blade relaxed its hold, and he sprawled there, rag-doll limp, among the debris of rumpled and stained table-linen and broken glass.

Such a tiny eruption of violence. Less noisy, by far, than any post-match rugby-team boisterousness. But lethal. Deadly. Horrific. And Jim, like a fallen giant, life-less and crooked-limbed, surrounded by external appendages of a wealth of which he'd been so proud. "The Skipper" . . . but also a "plumber" and also a "hit man". But for the moment that was forgotten. He was "The Skipper". Forty years before anti-aircraft shrapnel hadn't been able to kill him. This night three tiny bullets—bullets meant for killing crows and lesser vermin—had ended his life with small, but dramatic suddenness.

The unspoken realisation which seemed to fill the room with a sobering terror. If *he* could die so easily, *anybody* could.

Char bit hard upon the bent knuckle of a forefinger. Keith stared, almost with disbelief, at what had been the man he'd voted for to die. Ron closed his eyes, opened them again, then wiped the back of a hand across parched lips.

The hush seemed to last forever.

When Emily spoke her voice was a little hoarse, but brisk and business-like. But it was a false briskness; a briskness which wasn't far from being brittle, with the likelihood that it would crack at any moment.

"Keith. Collect Ada, then go to your room and pack. Ron. Your car's still at Preston?"

Ron nodded.

"Keith will give you a lift, I'm sure. To Preston. Anywhere."

"Sure," croaked Keith.

"The four of you. Out of here." She glanced at her wristwatch. "You'll get in somewhere. Some decent hotel, if you don't want to go home until morning. Just pack your bags and go. I'll have a word. Nobody will stop you."

Ron said, "What about you?"

"I'll be all right. These—these things have happened before."

"But it's *Jim*."

"To you." She swallowed. "To us. To them . . . it's just one more job. One more slight inconvenience to handle."

39

The Widow

IT was well past midnight. The other four had left. In the manager's office the two men—the men who'd been in the pin-table arcade—were explaining certain facts of life to that startled gentleman; dialling telephone numbers and allowing him to check and double-check that he'd *better* allow them to take over for the next few hours.

In the Cavern Room Emily Bathurst waited. She allowed tears the freedom to flow. Not a wailing. Not a heartbreak. Just a gentle, steady trickle as she moved around using her hands in order to keep the full impact from her mind. Straightening chairs. Lifting and closing the flick-blade, then placing it carefully alongside the corpse. Righting a fallen champagne bottle.

What she'd done had been necessary. More than necessary. Vital. Jim had broken the rules; he'd tried to recruit Keith; he'd boasted of his activities since leaving the RAF. He'd opened a door which should have remained locked. He'd *started* it, all *she'd* done was fill in the details. Scare tactics, perhaps? Or something else?

She lowered herself onto a chair and slowly lighted a cigarette.

She spoke, quietly, to a dead man. He couldn't hear, nevertheless he deserved something of an explanation.

"What else, Jim? I promised obedience, till death. Almost forty years ago. Till death. I kept my promise." She drew on the cigarette, and her hand shook. "You're still Jim," she whispered. "Still the *old* Jim. A flyer . . . not a killer. That you *shouldn't* have done. It wasn't worthy of you. The old Jim? He'd have been ashamed. Believe me . . . ashamed. As ashamed as I am."

She lowered her head, smoked the cigarette and waited. Knowing what would come next. The lined laundry basket. The van. The cleaning away of every sign. Then . . . nothing.

Already, he didn't exist. There'd be no marker, no headstone, not even a token burial service. Nothing! Perhaps a splash out there in the Irish Sea. If so, he wouldn't be washed ashore. These men were professionals; they didn't make silly mistakes like that. Just the sea and the fishes . . . like Tom and Karl, like Pete and Mark.

"Appropriate, Jim," she murmured, as if the corpse had read her thoughts. "It's where you sent *them*."

Meanwhile, she wished she could forget. She wished the mind was like a tap, to be turned on or off at will. To forget everything. To forget this last annual get-together, and all the other get-togethers. To forget her agony as she'd squeezed the trigger. To forget the passion with which, forty years before, she'd nursed a wounded man back to life. To forget the war. Everything!

But the mind didn't work that way. The mind was a vast storehouse of memories. Good, bad, frightening, wonderful, sweet, terrifying . . . more hues, more shades, than the world itself possessed. A world inside the head. A world in which time and space were meaningless. A world of here and now, superimposed upon a world of anywhere and always.

For Emily Bathurst at that moment a world of present tears and past might-have-beens.

40

The Motorway

A MOTORWAY in the small hours is a haunted place and none is more haunted than the M6. Despite the dipped beams, despite the oncoming lights of traffic in the north-bound lanes, despite the rise and fall of interior illumination from vehicles overtaking or being overtaken, the eeriness lasts from midnight to cockcrow. A gigantic, thousand-mile-long ghost train. A never-ending plunge into blackness with the cat's eyes rushing towards you like tracer bullets. Great conurbations of industry and inhabitation, picked out in lanes and roads of coloured lights, but not of the motorway and detached from the motorway. Lower than the motorway and adding to the unreal atmosphere; giving the impression that, despite the gentle road noise, the Cortina was low-flying. A modern witch's broomstick skimming the roofs of a slumbering land.

"*Why are we going home*?" asked Ada for the sixth time.

"Don't ask," pleaded Keith . . . also for the sixth time.

"Why did we drop Ron and Char off at Preston?"

"Because *they're* going home, as soon as they can collect their car."

"But, *why?*"

"Ada." He stared ahead with eyes which didn't seem quite sane. The set of his face was plain enough to see in the dim reflection from the dashboard light. "Ada, I'm changing jobs."

"I don't see what . . ."

"Farming."

"What?"

"Farming. It's a farming county. I'll farm. Anything. A change of houses."

"A change of jobs? A change of house?"

He nodded. A single movement of the head.

"Because—because of what happened back there?"

"You know enough about farming. You'll show me. I'll learn."

"Great heavens, what *did* happen back there?"

"You'll show me," he repeated.

"Keith, you're not . . ." She closed her mouth. The sentence couldn't be completed without hurt.

"Not young any more?"

"You're too old to change jobs."

"Dammit, I'll learn. If you won't show me, somebody else will."

"Farming. It takes a lifetime of experience. It can't be just—y'know—*taught*."

"A smallholding then."

"It's not easy, Keith. You read books about it. All this modern back-to-earth rubbish. It's far more difficult than they make it sound."

"Other people do it. I'll do it. *We'll* do it."

"You have a job. A good job."

"I want to be with you as much as possible."

"That's nice of you," she said gently, "but . . ."

"I don't want to leave you alone."

"You mean . . ." she paused, then ended, "*unprotected*?"

He remained silent. Refused to be drawn.

Suddenly the darkness rushed away from them, and they seemed to be hurtling through a saffron-drenched maze. Amber lights whipped past overhead. Dual- and three-lane carriageways peeled off in the visual equivalent of disappearing screams. Other motorways ran parallel, on concrete stilts; an architecture of futuristic madness. They seemed to be racing along a cat's cradle of yellow-tinged surfaces. Girdered bridges carried lighted warning of the approaching junction with the M5 and below, in a great hollow of darkness, the lights of Walsall and West Bromwich reached out for the greater mass of lights which pin-pointed Birmingham.

"Need we go so fast?" she murmured.

"I want to get home."

"Home?"

"Back to sanity."

"Or away from where we've left?"

She saw the wetness building up on the surface of his eyes, and had sense enough to remain silent until his composure returned.

Until the amber madness was behind them and, once more, they were travelling along unlit motorway.

"Those men," she ventured at last.

"Which men?"

"When Emily told me to telephone. The two men who joined me in the lounge."

He grunted.

"They looked hard men," she said. "Policemen, I thought. The sort of policemen who handle major crime."

"Not policemen," he murmured.

"Criminals?" She turned her head to watch his face. "They could have been criminals, I suppose. Top-line criminals. It's hard to tell one from the other."

"Don't." His voice was harsh with misery.

"Don't what?"

"Remember them. Remember what they looked like. Remember anything about them."

"Why not?"

"Just don't . . . that's all. Forget it ever happened."

"Keith." Her tone admitted no argument. "I'm your wife, remember? No secrets. Earlier—yesterday afternoon—you confessed the biggest secret possible, and I forced myself to understand. It wasn't easy. *But no more secrets*. Otherwise . . ." She shook her head slowly. "I have to know, Keith. I'll not live with you in ignorance. I couldn't!"

"It's not the same thing."

"That's what you say, but how do I know unless you tell me?"

"All right." Again the single nod, and a deep, shuddering sigh. "The next Services stop, we'll pull off the road. I'll tell you. Just the once, but no more. No questions. No explanations. Enough to let you know. After that . . . never again, so don't ask."

They'd passed junction four and, after some miles more of motoring, Keith slowed the car and swung left up the slip-road and into the services stop. He followed the signs to the car-park and found an isolated, darkened corner. He braked the car, switched off the ignition, then lighted a cigarette.

The lights from the all-night cafe didn't reach them. In the distance—in the lorry-park—massive vehicles were parked and waiting to continue their long journeys.

Shadowy figures moved to and from the lighted entrance to the cafe, but they were far enough away to neither see nor hear. It was the most private place in the world—or so it seemed—and what he said was, despite the awkwardness of the telling, the most private secret of the world.

"I—I saved his life. Forty years ago. You know why. He told you. I told *them*. The truth. I saved his life . . . by default." He smoked the cigarette jerkily. The sentences wouldn't come smoothly or even in proper sequence. "I saved his life. I keep telling myself that. It doesn't excuse things. But it helps. That *I* saved his life."

"Jim?" She allowed herself the single-word question.

"I had the right. Dammit, if anybody had the right, *I* had the right." He stumbled forward, fighting to convince himself. To excuse himself. He wound down the window to allow the cigarette smoke to laze its way through the slot above his right shoulder. "I voted. That's all. I voted because, in effect, she was asking whether he'd wasted his life . . . and he *had*. Killing people. I don't give a damn why. I don't give a damn what fancy name they call it. *Killing people* . . ."

"*Jim!*"

"She said 'vote', and I voted. God! I didn't think she *meant* it. Bluff. Maybe to make him change his ways. Maybe to scare him. But not to *mean* it. Not *seriously* . . ."

"Keith, I don't know what . . ."

"She shot him. She shot *Jim*. Because I voted, see? Me and Char . . ."

"You and Char?"

"She asked for a show of hands. Then —then she shot him. And—and—and I didn't want *that*. Good God! If I'd thought she meant it. Lousy. Sure . . . lousy. A government killer. A hit man. He'd even tried to recruit *me* into . . ." He shook his head in near-disbelief. "But she *shouldn't*."

"You mean," she asked gently, "you were there when somebody murdered Jim?"

"Emily," he whispered.

"In that case, shouldn't we . . ."

"No." His voice was flat and expressionless. "Forget it now. *Please*. The men you sent for. The two men. There'll—there'll be no police enquiry. No murder charge. Nothing! It's—it's all under control. Just that—just that you saw them. It scares me. We need to move house. Just in case. A farm. A smallholding. Out in the wilds somewhere. And—and I daren't leave you alone. How in hell can we be sure? But we *have* to be. We can't go through life . . ." He widened the window opening, threw out what was left of the cigarette, took great gulps of air, then said, "That's it, then. No more questions. No more arguments. Nothing. I won't listen. I won't answer. These last two days . . . we forget them. Completely. Everything. A small farm—a smallholding, maybe—with a cottage attached. I won't be talked out of it. No more hawking knick-knacks. No more junk-shops. We draw a line, see? No more Hellen, no more Char, no more Emily, no more Ron. No more anybody or anything. Just us two, and sod the rest. That's how it's going to be from now on."

He wound up the window, started the car and nosed it from the shadow of the car-park; down the slip-road and back onto the motorway. He drove less furiously than before. More relaxed. As if some unknown terror had left him.

Ada leaned back in her seat and closed her eyes. She had the wisdom of her sex; the wisdom of her kind. A line *had* been drawn, and she knew she'd never know every detail above that line . . . or ever *want* to know.

41

The By-Pass

IT was a good garage. The Jag was as good as new; sweet-purring and with every horse under the bonnet ready to respond to the slightest pressure on the accelerator. Ron paid the bill and was satisfied. He eased the car over the pavement and across the line of traffic, then pointed the nose east.

They'd stayed what had been left of the night in a good hotel. A double-bed for the first time in years. No love-making; they'd been too tired—too mentally and emotionally exhausted—for love-making, but they each knew that would come later. Not as wild as once-upon-a-time, perhaps. But it would come. Gentler, deeper, more precious. It would come.

They'd slept in each other's arms. A silent promise and a form of protection. They'd awakened in time to hear the early news on the radio, but there'd been no mention of the Cave Hotel. Not even a hint. They'd bought morning newspapers—national and local—but although they'd searched every page, they'd found no report of a murder at Lytham St. Annes.

"The police?" Char had asked in amazement. "Are *they* in it?"

"I doubt it. It's something—y'know—beyond the scope of the police."

"But surely . . ."

"The police only know there's been a killing, if they're told or if they find the body."

"I—I suppose so."

"Gag everybody. Remove the corpse. What do the police know?"

And they'd left it at that. What else? They were too involved—far too involved—to raise a dust storm. They'd eaten their breakfast, packed their bags, paid the bill and ordered a taxi to the garage.

And now they were on the by-pass which wasn't a by-pass. Trying to time the traffic lights. Being jostled into the wrong lane, then being held up by vehicles parked at the kerb.

Char said, "Keith should be home by now."

"Should be."

"I wish to hell *we* were."

Ron remained silent, concentrating upon keeping the Jag moving forward until they were on the A59, past the twin roundabouts and on the dual carriageway. Then he relaxed a little and spoke.

"We'll never really know," he sighed.

"What?"

"Why she did it. Why this year and not before."

"He'd called you names. You and Keith. He'd called you names, even though you saved his life."

"No." Ron kept his attention on the road ahead, but shook his head. "More than that. It takes more than that."

"He'd turned rogue," she suggested. "Killer."

"She knew. She'd lived with it."

"She was a nurse, remember that. *She'd* helped to save his life, too. Nursing. Killing. They don't go together. There's a limit. He passed that limit."

"But not last night," argued Ron. "Last night he was the Jim we all knew . . . or thought we knew. Bombastic. A little drunk. So *why last night*?"

"He called you names." She dropped a hand onto his knee. It was as if she wished to make the newly-found communication more complete. "Emily thought a lot about you, darling. Both you and Keith, but especially you."

"That's no reason for murder," he muttered. "Dammit, that's no reason at all. A drunk, mouthing stupidities. That's all it boiled down to."

"You didn't vote," she said gently.

"No."

"Why not?"

"Christ! All right, let's be dramatic, you don't save a man's life then vote for his execution." He paused, then added, "You did."

"Uh-huh."

"Why?"

"It's—er—hard to say. Hard to explain." She removed the hand from his knee. "Keith voted. Keith knew him, better than I did. I suppose I followed suit. Dammit, he'd said some lousy things about both of you." She hesitated, then said, "I think I thought she was bluffing."

"Bluffing?"

"Waving that silly gun around. Such a *little* gun . . ."

"Guns are made to kill."

"I thought she was trying to sober him up. Scare him a little after all the things he'd said."

"Men like Jim don't scare."

"No, well, we all know that *now*."

"I wish you hadn't voted," he said softly.

She looked sad, but resigned. She made no reply to the remark.

The Jag wound its way along the A59, climbing up to the top of the Pennines; across "the Backbone of England" and from one rose county into another. The moorland looked wild and never-ending; eternity to eternity, in which the death of one man counted for less than nothing.

They'd left Skipton behind and were dropping down the eastern slopes, towards Harrogate, when she next spoke.

"All these years," she mused. "You've tormented yourself about the four that jumped."

"I could have stopped it." His voice was deadpan, but weary. "I had the rank. We might *all* have been saved."

"You weren't to know."

"No." The quick smile was twisted and mirthless. "As you say . . . all these years. Pete and Karl and Mark and Tom. I can't even *remember* them other than as names. As members of the crew. I've often tried to remember their faces, but I can't. That's terrible."

"Forty years. It's a long time. If Keith had jumped . . . the same thing, surely?"

"I suppose," he sighed.

She waited a moment, then said, "You'd have gone down with him."

"What?"

"Jim. You were with him. *He* couldn't jump, but you'd have gone down with him."

"It didn't happen." His tone was awkward and embarrassed.

"But as far as you *knew*. It was *going* to happen."

He nodded slowly.

"Dying with him," she breathed.

"With that wound. Hell, I couldn't *leave* him." He suddenly laughed, quietly and with a touch of hysteria. "Bloody stupid. Of them all—of all the crew—I liked *him* least."

"If there's a hero . . ." she began.

"No heroes."

"You're the one. You deliberately chose to . . ."

"No heroes!" he repeated sharply. Then, in a gentler tone, "Char, it wasn't heroic. None of it. War isn't like that, except on the TV or in books. On a cinema screen, maybe. Bravery? Degrees of terror, that's all. You try to swallow it. If you do and it doesn't choke you, you're a 'hero'. You might even get a medal. But, basically, you're no braver than the next guy. The guy who ran away. The guy who jumped. That's the con, darling. That there are cowards and heroes on *either* side. Idiots! All of them, idiots. Grown men—more often than not decent men—killing each other—killing women and kids—because those at the top are either mad or weak. And we, the idiots, put them there." He took a deep breath, then ended, "Wars start at tables, darling. World leaders can't agree . . . they haven't the common gumption to meet each other half-way. Crazy. Because wars *end* at tables, and this time they *have* to agree. Why the hell couldn't they in the first place? What's so damn wonderful about killing or being killed?

What does it *prove*? Not that one side's right or the other side's wrong. Just that—that . . ."

He ran out of words and compressed his lips in disgust.

"Cool it, my pet." She dropped a hand to his knee again. "It's a wonderful belief. Hold on to it. It's one of the things that make you a very complete man . . . and me a fool for not recognising it before now."

42

The Hotel

THE Cave Hotel, Lytham St. Annes. It tops the lot; forget every other hotel or eating establishment within even moderate driving distance.

It now has the only thing it once lacked. A secret. And what a secret!

The Savoy, Claridge's, The Ritz—all the great hotels of the capital, all the great hotels of the world—carry their own secrets and are justifiably proud of the fact that those secrets are as closely guarded as the Crown jewels. Nobody tells. Other than a handful of people, nobody ever knows. There is no record. What happened is not even passed from mouth to mouth there-fore, as men die, so the secrets die.

It can be argued that this is one of the many things which *makes* a great hotel great. Limitless confidentiality. Knowledge, on the part of those who need such knowledge, that it is "safe".

And word gets around. Nothing specific—no hint of the why or wherefore—merely a dropped hint in the right ear from the right lips, that such-and-such a place is "reliable". In the world of whispers, that's all it needs. Quite suddenly the place becomes "off limits" as far as normal police supervision is concerned. The supervision is taken over by quiet men, with hard eyes and limitless power; the staff are questioned, without even knowing they are being questioned; chosen rooms are re-decorated and re-furnished, and what happens in those rooms becomes the subject of careful scrutiny at regular intervals; tapes are listened to, then filed away, negatives from hidden, pin-point cameras are developed, scrutinised, then pigeon-holed for possible future reference.

It is a dirty business—some might say a grossly unfair business, in that the privacy of the innocent is no more sacrosanct than the privacy of the guilty—but it is a business which is as necessary as is the rôle of men paid to do what James Bathurst was paid to do. The game—deadly, dirty and unfair though it is—is played by every nation under the sun, and to opt out of the game is to risk eventual annihilation. The Cave Hotel is now part of the playing area of that game.

You may, if you wish and if the management approve, still reserve the Cavern Room for some private function. But do not expect to find bullet scars on the table or blood marks on the carpet. It is still, primarily, a class hotel. Most of its guests are decent, ordinary people, a little better heeled than the average . . . and "the others" you wouldn't recognise anyway.

43

The Restaurant

LONDON is not merely the capital city of the United Kingdom. It is also the capital city of the world. In no other city will you find the headquarters or sub-headquarters of as many terrorist organisations, guerrilla groups, off-beat anarchist cartels, displaced heads of state planning counter-coups or general collections of homicidally-minded lunatics. London is the Mecca of madmen. Like flies attracted to the slumbering form of a gorged tiger, they are attracted by the epitome of a democracy they will never understand and could never tolerate. That they are "allowed" is enough. They waste no time on pondering the reason for being "allowed".

However . . .

Democracy, like every other priceless gem, has to be guarded, and the guardians must be as sly and as ruthless as those who wish to destroy it. Democracy very often says "You may" which in turn, is translated by fools into "You must" and, at that point, the guardians step in and very firmly say "You may *not*". The spoilers step beyond the law and, to reach them, the guardians must often follow. A dangerous circle, trodden by dangerous men. Yet, outwardly, some of them do not *look* dangerous.

The man murmured, "I'm sorry, my dear."

"Is it important?" Emily Bathurst carefully placed her knife and fork along the centre of her plate. The food had been good and perfectly prepared and presented, but she hadn't really tasted it. "It was a limited choice. I made it."

Most of the other customers were men; businessmen, lunching with clients and, perhaps, out to make an impression. It was that sort of restaurant. Expensive. Select. Hidden away in one of the side-streets within easy walking distance of Fleet Street and the various Inns of Court. The conversation was a low murmur. Each table an island of privacy and far enough from its neighbours to ensure that accidental eaves-dropping was very unlikely.

Nevertheless, what was said was meaningless, other than to Emily and the man.

"He was," sighed the man, "very garrulous."

"Unfortunately."

"He *had* been warned. I, personally, spoke to him. Explained the situation. It was becoming rather embarrassing."

"He was that sort of man."

"Unfortunately."

At sight, the man looked like an army officer in mufti. From the Brigade of Guards, perhaps. The immaculate cut of the quiet, clerical-grey suit, complete with waistcoat. The white shirt and the regimental tie. The well-groomed hair which came only from a weekly trim. The clipped moustache which he fingered gently now and then. He'd left his curled brolly and bowler at the cloakroom.

It was easy to imagine him giving words of advice to some junior officer new to regimental discipline.

"A rule of life, my boy. A good bowel movement before you start the day. Keeps you fit and ready for anything."

He swayed slightly to one side as the waiter collected his empty plate. Then the waiter took Emily's plate, too.

"Coffee, madam?"

"Yes, please. Black."

"Black for me, too," said the man.

The waiter left them, and the man said, "The others?"

Emily hesitated, then said, "They don't know much."

"Nevertheless . . ." The man made the single word mean as much as a complete sentence.

Emily didn't answer.

The ritual of pouring and sweetening coffee was performed in silence. The man opened a cigarette case, offered it to Emily, then took a cigarette himself. When they were smoking and sipping coffee, he spoke again.

"There's the possibility he may have said something."

"It's possible," she agreed sadly.

"He was something of a braggart."

"I'm afraid so."

"Therefore . . ." Again the single word which conveyed so much.

"Have I a say in the matter?" she asked heavily.

"You can express an opinion."

"They're nice people."

He drew on the cigarette and remarked, "Most people are nice people."

"What I mean is . . ."

"I know exactly what you mean, my dear." He smiled. "*He* was a nice person, but he had a weakness."

She breathed, "Oh, my God!"

"Leave it to me," he soothed. "There'll be a decision. One way or the other. Don't worry. It's out of your hands."

She looked infinitely sad.

"Take a rest," he advised. "A long rest. I'll see you're not required for some considerable time."

44

Loose Ends

RON died within the month.

He had a short period of once-upon-a-time happiness with Char, then there was a road accident. A lorry forced the Jag from the road as they climbed the hill towards the Pennine Moors. A business trip. Somebody had telephoned enquiring about the possibility of putting one of the high and wild farmsteads onto the market. The property had to be seen and valued.

He never reached the farmstead. The Jag rolled and cartwheeled into the ravine, but without the Technicolor ball of flame beloved of film-makers. Instead, a dead driver with a broken back, along with half the other bones of his body.

The police never traced the lorry. Come to that—and after the funeral—nobody ever traced either the caller or the farmstead.

Something of a mystery, it was concluded. One of those silly, hoax telephone messages with tragic consequences.

Char died little more than a week after burying Ron.

Poor Char. Broken-hearted and unable to face prolonged widowhood, she took her own life. An overdose of Seconal . . . that's what the pathologist said. The doctor gave evidence that he'd warned her never to take more than two capsules at a time. Two before she retired, and never with strong liquor. The pathologist gave evidence of the stomach contents. The remains of at least a dozen Seconal capsules, and the equivalent of three double whiskies.

The two sons were quietly surprised at this close bond between their parents. Privately, they'd thought the marriage to be on the rocks.

Back at the house, after the inquest, the door-bell rang. The younger son answered.

The Electricity Board man said, "Read your meter, sir."

"It's already been read." The younger son looked surprised.

"No, sir." The meter man consulted his book. "Not this quarter, sir."

"The other day." The younger man swallowed. "The day my mother died . . ."

"I'm sorry to hear about that, sir."

"I let him in. I had an appointment I couldn't break. I was going out when the van came in at the gate. I *know*. Two days ago. It's already *been* read."

"Sorry, sir." The meter reader looked embarrassed. "They're always swopping and changing around. We get it sometimes. A new man doesn't know the exact boundaries of his area." He chewed his lower lip, then said, "I can come back, if you like. If it isn't convenient."

"No, it's not that. But . . ."

"There's no record of it having been read, sir."

"All right. I suppose . . ." The younger man sighed. "You'd better come in and read it again."

"Thank you, sir."

Keith re-hooked the receiver and said, "Damn!"

"Isn't he coming?" asked Ada.

"The damn fool's lost, somewhere

between here and Layham." Keith moved across the farmhouse kitchen, pulled on gumboots and thrust his arms into the sleeves of a donkey-jacket as he continued. "He's sorry, but he'd like his sow covered by the boar. Specifically *our* boar. He's heard it's from a good strain."

"So it is. And the money would come in useful."

"I'll find the fool."

Keith stomped from the house and a few moments later Ada heard the ancient Land Rover grind into life.

She loved that man. God, how she loved him! He had more down-to-earth common-or-garden guts than any man or woman she'd ever met.

This farm . . . little more than an enlarged smallholding. He'd sold his house, most of his home and damn near his soul. But he'd bought it. A tiny area of the county, hidden away miles from anywhere. And he wasn't the dreamer she'd thought him to be. A knock-down price for land which had been farmed almost to death. He'd accepted it, and planned accordingly.

"It's no good thinking about growing anything for two or three years . . . Let the soil recover . . . Feed it and let it rest . . . It won't even grow decent grass at the moment . . . We'll concentrate on pigs and chickens for a few years . . . Bacon and eggs. At least we won't starve . . . Those piggeries. I can do running repairs, then build up a nice herd . . . We'll stick to pigs and hens until we can grow spuds then, what potatoes we can't either sell or eat ourselves, we can feed to the pigs."

Logic. Small-farm logic. It had called for graft—sunrise-to-sunset graft—but and despite his age he'd never once complained. First the piggeries. Then a careful selection of stock. Nor had he been proud. He'd sought advice from pig men and, having been given that advice, he'd considered it and, after careful thought, taken most of it. Already they were breaking even. They could live. They could afford to *allow* the land to recover. No luxuries, of course, but in five years' time . . .

The boar had been his idea.

"Not too many boars about. It's a good boar—a *very* good boar—and it's dirt cheap. They'll come for miles to have their sows covered. It'll help. Either straight cash or a couple from the litter."

Certainly the boar had been cheap. More than that, among the pig fraternity, it was known. The sire of some magnificent litters . . . but what an evil beast!

The day they'd delivered it . . .

"Take it easy, mister. I'd trust this bugger as far as I'd trust Old Nick."

"Keep that pitchfork low, mister. He'll be under it, else, and he'll have one of your legs off."

"Get in that pen, you black-souled bastard. Christ! You be careful when you're handling this old bugger, mister. He's nasty. *Bloody* nasty."

And this from a man born and brought up with pigs.

From its day of arrival Ada had been terrified of the boar. It was never allowed to leave its pen; to give it greater freedom than the walls of its pen allowed would have been too dangerous. She knew enough about boars. The bad ones. Bulls were gentle creatures by comparison. It watched you. Followed you with its eyes. Waiting for the slightest drop of guard. Ready with those great yellow teeth. Charging the heavy gate in a mad rush each time you came near.

Muscular malignancy on four powerful legs.

And yet it had already more than paid for both its purchase and its keep. It had been a good investment. Its blind, savage virility was something to marvel at.

Less than an hour later she heard the Land Rover return. There was the sound of a second car and the occasional bump and creak of a small trailer. Pig squeals from the direction of the pens. A silence followed by the sound of the car and trailer leaving.

She stayed in the farmhouse kitchen. This was one aspect of farming she left to Keith. Necessary, of course, necessary. But man's work. No decent, self-respecting woman wanted to stand gawking at animals mating.

Keith didn't return to the house. Obviously, he was feeding the pigs while he was there. Why not? It would save him from doing the job later.

But he was taking his time . . .

As dusk approached she took the powerful electric torch and went in search of him. It was gloomy in the pens at the best of times. She heard the nuzzling and the crunching—the slobbering and the sucking—as she drew near. It came from the boar's pen. It was a physical effort to raise and aim the beam of the torch . . . and then she saw it.

The boar's mask. Snout and cheeks scarlet, and mouth dripping blood. The front trotters crimson from where they'd stood. The tiny eyes gleaming as if in foul triumph. And, littered around the floor of the pen, the torn and mangled mess that had once been . . . that had once been . . . that had once been . . .

She screamed as she fainted, but she didn't hear herself scream.

The London-based specialist pronounced solemn and final verdict. The two men —Keith's brother and Ada's brother— listened, believed and were shocked.

"I'm afraid there's little hope. Very little hope indeed." He spread his spatulate fingers on the glass-covered top of the desk, and spoke slowly and carefully, in order that they both understood. "The mind is a very delicate thing. Like a beautifully made clock. Smash such a clock with, say, a sledge-hammer and it's well beyond repair.

The same with her mind. Modern drugs, modern techniques, can do many things, but there's a limit. She's beyond that limit. Well beyond that limit. She doesn't know who she is. She isn't even able to appreciate that she's a living creature. I don't think she ever will."

He sighed, waited until the import of what he'd said had registered, then continued, "We'll not experiment. That I promise you. She can't differentiate between comfort and discomfort but, despite this, she'll be made as comfortable as possible. Kept as comfortable as possible. Again, you have my word." Another pause. Another wait until the full horror was digested. "You may, of course, visit her. I'll be blunt . . . if you *do* visit her it will merely be as a salve to your own consciences. She won't recognise you. Either of you. She'll never recognise anybody ever again. She'll never remember anything. She'll never know who she is or where she is. In layman terms her mind has ceased to function. Like the clock. It will never work again. My considered opinion, after every test *I* know of. The body is alive. The mind is dead. Eventually the body will waste away. A shocking prospect, I know, but I'd be less than honest if I held out any hope at all." Another pause. Another wait. "You may, of course, seek a second opinion . . ."

"No, it's . . ." Ada's brother licked his lips. He looked to be in a state of shock as, indeed, did Keith's brother. He croaked, "That's—that's all right. No second opinion. She's—y'know— just look after her. That's all. That's all we *can* do."

"Unfortunately," agreed the specialist sadly.

The man bringing his sow? The man who'd "lost his way" between Layham and the Parkinson farmstead?

There was no record of him ever having existed. As simple and as terrifying as that. The incident shocked the neighbourhood, but nobody had any doubts. That damn boar was a rogue animal. Known as such. Sold cheaply for just that reason. Keith Parkinson had been careless. It was a terrible thing to happen—of course it was a terrible thing to happen—and, when she'd seen what the boar had done to her husband, the sight had turned Ada

Parkinson's mind. A terrible, terrible thing to happen.

But what to do?

Put the bloody boar down, fast!

Then try to forget it. Otherwise you'll never trust another boar in your life.

45

The Recluse

TAKE the A390 from Gunnislake to Liskeard. A mere eight miles and, for stretches of those eight miles, the sea west of Plymouth can be seen across the fields, about six miles away. It can be seen, if it is fine weather. Seen clearly. But if it *is* fine weather you're in luck. The chances are that it will be either raining or misty. Cornwall—especially along the south coast—a land of rain and a land of mist. A land of strange beliefs and even stranger truths. They will tell you the boy Jesus trod British soil, east of the Tamar. No—not British soil—*Celtic* soil. The Cornishman holds the firm belief that he is not of England; that beyond the Tamar is a land foreign to his blood; that the Jew, Joseph of Arimathea sailed his merchant voyages, landed on the Cornish coast and that, on at least one occasion, he brought with him his small nephew . . . Jesus of

Nazareth. Cornwall, then. A holy land. A haunted land. A mysterious land.

Take the A390 from Gunnislake to Liskeard and on the left, the sea. On average a mere half-dozen miles away. But within those half-dozen miles—within that forty-odd square miles of countryside—more tiny hamlets, more hidden inlets, more high-hedged lanes than a non-Cornish mind can encompass. Quethiock. Menheniot. Polbathic. Cornish names given to clusters of dwellings. Hamlets, and small hamlets at that. But they are almost lost inside that web of narrow, single-track lanes. But there are also houses, cottages, bungalows which belong to nowhere. They are just *there*. Lonely and isolated. Unknown and unseen behind high banks topped by blackthorn.

Perfect hiding places . . . or so thought Emily Bathurst.

Jim had been wise. Cunning. Perhaps he had realised his own weakness and, if he had, he had also known that such weaknesses are not tolerated. A bolt-hole, then. An all-mod-con hideaway within reasonable running distance of the Big City.

She could have warned him. Oh, yes,

she'd already tormented herself long and often on that score. She could have warned him that the plumbers had been detailed to flush one of their own number. But would he have believed her? His arrogance was monumental. He might have laughed at the idea. Even had he believed, he might have defied any man to kill him before he killed the would-be-killer. The sort of man he was. God! It would have added spice to life. To be hunted, knowing he was being hunted, then spreading a trap for the hunters.

But he *would* have been killed . . . eventually.

As a warning to others, perhaps. As an example. Therefore, not a clean death. Not even a quick death. Something special. Something to make grown men shudder. To make them think twice before even hinting that, beyond the known boundaries of officialdom, there was a never-ending battlefield in which terror and counter-terror wrestled for the upper hand.

So long ago—it seemed so very long ago—she'd pleaded for his quick death. Not his life. That would have been asking too much. Merely that he be allowed to die quickly. Cleanly. Without prolonged pain. Without being made to scream for a death which was being deliberately withheld.

"I'll do it myself." The choking desperation with which she'd made that terrible promise.

"*You?*"

"When he's not expecting it. Please!"

"Can we trust you?"

"Do you ever trust anybody?" Then, having voiced the cynicism, "Yes, you can trust me. He's done good work for you in the past . . ."

"True."

"At least grant him this small mercy."

"That his wife should flush him?"

"That he not be allowed to *know*. He'll be no less dead."

It had taken thirty minutes of arguing. Thirty minutes of desperate pleading.

Then a curt, "Not too long. If we think you're taking too long, we'll step in. You won't know when. Just . . . soon."

These men. These official assassins. They were like mechanical humanoids. Hand-picked, then brainwashed. They *had* to be. No emotion. Expressionless eyes. Devoid of every last vestige of humanity.

They killed or arranged killings. That was their job. Their profession. They performed their duties as naturally, as easily, as a well-trained drill squad. Scores of ways of taking life, and masking it as "accidental death". They knew them all. Every terror organisation in the world feared them . . . and with cause!

But she'd won her plea.

Then had come the agony. A hundred times she could have killed him without his knowledge. A hundred times . . . *more* than a hundred times. A score of times each day. Every night while he was asleep in bed. Every time he'd turned his back on her. He wouldn't have known. He wouldn't have felt a thing.

But in cold blood!

Odd. Had the roles been reversed, *he* could have done it. She had no misconceptions. Jim. Professionalism personified. Had the roles been reversed, there'd have been a single shot. Unseen, unknown; hopefully, unfelt. A job to be done, and he'd have done it.

But with her that extra boost had been necessary. An argument. A deliberately forced sense of outrage. A contrived anger.

It had been *necessary*. And that first shot had missed, therefore, he'd known. His final awareness had been that his wife was about to murder him.

Dear God! Dear, sweet Jesus!

She sat alone in the gloom of the cottage, and tormented herself with recent memories and wondered whether they'd ever move from the front of her mind.

Her whole body jerked as the doorbell rang.

She rose from the chair, pulled on the curtains, switched on the lights and answered the ring. She half-expected him and he was there. The man with the military bearing; the immaculately dressed, quietly spoken officer-type. He was wearing a mac and as he stepped, uninvited, into the cottage, he casually unbelted the mac until it swung loosely from his shoulders.

As she closed the door, he looked around approvingly, and said, "What a charming place."

Without answering, she led the way into the lounge and gestured with a hand for him to sit on one of the deep armchairs. He lowered himself, eased the crease of his trousers, then crossed his legs. He waited until she, too, was settled in another armchair before he spoke.

"Where James planned to retire, I take it?"

"Something like that."

Her tone was flat and expressionless. She'd finished running. Finished worrying. Finished *living*.

"My dear," he said gently. Chidingly. "You made something of a hash of things, wouldn't you agree?"

"It wasn't easy."

"It never is."

"Not as easy as I thought it would be."

"But—pardon me—your choice?"

"My choice," she breathed.

"And badly done."

"I'm not an expert."

"Quite. But that, too, should have been taken into consideration."

"Are you here to slap my wrist?" A sad half-smile accompanied the question.

"Something like that."

He reached into the inside pocket of his jacket for a cigarette case. He didn't offer her one. Having lighted it, he returned the lighter to his side pocket and produced the pistol.

"Custom-made," he explained in a gentle, academic tone.

"Really?"

"Short barrel, built-on silencer." He drew on the cigarette. "Obviously a short-range weapon."

"Obviously," she mocked gently.

"Short-range, therefore half-charged cartridges. Combine the two and it's no louder than a man clearing his throat."

"That must be a great comfort."

"Special rounds," he drawled, as if she hadn't spoken. "Magnesium core. A tiny explosion on impact. A little like having a small incendiary bomb explode in the brain. Quite painless."

"In God's name, how can a man like . . ."

For a micro-second it felt as if she'd been struck on the forehead with a pile-driver. Then it was all over.

In effect, her shattered head seemed to be blazing. He didn't even look. He glanced at his wrist-watch, then removed two cylinders from his mac pocket. Silver-coloured cylinders, not much bigger than large fireworks. Each had a fuse. Quietly—calmly—he touched the end of each fuse with the glowing end of the cigarette. They began to smoulder, and he placed one cylinder near her side and the second cylinder not far from a plug socket in the skirting-board.

Then, he left the house, dropping the latch behind him, strolled down the path and began to walk along the lane. In less than a minute the car caught up with him, the front nearside door was opened from inside and, without waiting for the car to come to a complete halt, he swung himself inside.

The car gathered speed as he closed the door . . . and he might never have been in Cornwall.

Emily Bathurst's head still blazed and, as the fuses burned themselves out the haematite-based compound inside the cylinders roared into life. Heat capable of melting steel. In minutes, the cottage was a fireball and well beyond any hope of control.

The experts—the police and the fire service—puzzled over the problem. The possible cause of the fire. Eventually, they settled for a wiring fault . . . they had to say *something*!

The body—what was left of it—was never identified. Nobody knew her. Nobody missed her.

To be brutally honest, and shock apart, nobody even cared.

46

Susie

THE North Sea. South of the Norwegian Sea, north of the English Channel. Not too big and, by comparison with the great oceans of the world, not particularly deep. But don't let the statistics fool you. Deep enough and big enough and, at times, angry beyond its size.

Between '39 and '45 it developed a voracious appetite. It grew to like aeroplanes. Monoplanes, biplanes, single-engined, twin-engined, four-engined. Nor did the nationality of the aeroplane matter. It swallowed them all. Thousands! And, with them, their occupants.

Nobody knows how many. Nobody ever will know.

But one of them was a Lancaster bomber, wounded and struggling back towards its home base. The North Sea gulped four of the bomber's crew before the aircraft itself disappeared into its salty maw.

Three men fought it, and licked it, but they too are now dead. They and the three women who waited to marry them.

Somewhere in the sanded silt of the North Sea odd bits and pieces—unrecognisable bits and pieces—of Susie may well remain. It matters not.

The crew, like Susie, have ceased to exist.

Once upon a time, they were heroes . . . but no more.

THE END

This book is published under the
auspices of the
ULVERSCROFT FOUNDATION,
a registered charity, whose primary object is to assist those who experience difficulty in reading print of normal size.

In response to approaches from the medical world, the Foundation is also helping to purchase the latest, most sophisticated medical equipment desperately needed by major eye hospitals for the diagnosis and treatment of eye diseases.

If you would like to know more about the
ULVERSCROFT FOUNDATION,
and how you can help to further its work,
please write for details to:

THE ULVERSCROFT FOUNDATION
The Green, Bradgate Road
Anstey
Leicestershire
England

GUIDE
TO THE COLOUR CODING
OF
ULVERSCROFT BOOKS

Many of our readers have written to us expressing their appreciation for the way in which our colour coding has assisted them in selecting the Ulverscroft books of their choice.

To remind everyone of our colour coding—this is as follows:

BLACK COVERS
Mysteries

★

BLUE COVERS
Romances

★

RED COVERS
Adventure Suspense and General Fiction

★

ORANGE COVERS
Westerns

★

GREEN COVERS
Non-Fiction

MYSTERY TITLES
in the
Ulverscroft Large Print Series

Henrietta Who?	*Catherine Aird*
Slight Mourning	*Catherine Aird*
The China Governess	*Margery Allingham*
Coroner's Pidgin	*Margery Allingham*
Crime at Black Dudley	*Margery Allingham*
Look to the Lady	*Margery Allingham*
More Work for the Undertaker	*Margery Allingham*
Death in the Channel	*J. R. L. Anderson*
Death in the City	*J. R. L. Anderson*
Death on the Rocks	*J. R. L. Anderson*
A Sprig of Sea Lavender	*J. R. L. Anderson*
Death of a Poison-Tongue	*Josephine Bell*
Murder Adrift	*George Bellairs*
Strangers Among the Dead	*George Bellairs*
The Case of the Abominable Snowman	*Nicholas Blake*
The Widow's Cruise	*Nicholas Blake*
The Brides of Friedberg	*Gwendoline Butler*
Murder By Proxy	*Harry Carmichael*
Post Mortem	*Harry Carmichael*
Suicide Clause	*Harry Carmichael*
After the Funeral	*Agatha Christie*
The Body in the Library	*Agatha Christie*

A Caribbean Mystery	*Agatha Christie*
Curtain	*Agatha Christie*
The Hound of Death	*Agatha Christie*
The Labours of Hercules	*Agatha Christie*
Murder on the Orient Express	*Agatha Christie*
The Mystery of the Blue Train	*Agatha Christie*
Parker Pyne Investigates	*Agatha Christie*
Peril at End House	*Agatha Christie*
Sleeping Murder	*Agatha Christie*
Sparkling Cyanide	*Agatha Christie*
They Came to Baghdad	*Agatha Christie*
Third Girl	*Agatha Christie*
The Thirteen Problems	*Agatha Christie*
The Black Spiders	*John Creasey*
Death in the Trees	*John Creasey*
The Mark of the Crescent	*John Creasey*
Quarrel with Murder	*John Creasey*
Two for Inspector West	*John Creasey*
His Last Bow	*Sir Arthur Conan Doyle*
The Valley of Fear	*Sir Arthur Conan Doyle*
Dead to the World	*Francis Durbridge*
My Wife Melissa	*Francis Durbridge*
Alive and Dead	*Elizabeth Ferrars*
Breath of Suspicion	*Elizabeth Ferrars*
Drowned Rat	*Elizabeth Ferrars*
Foot in the Grave	*Elizabeth Ferrars*

Murders Anonymous	*Elizabeth Ferrars*
Don't Whistle 'Macbeth'	*David Fletcher*
A Calculated Risk	*Rae Foley*
The Slippery Step	*Rae Foley*
This Woman Wanted	*Rae Foley*
Home to Roost	*Andrew Garve*
The Forgotten Story	*Winston Graham*
Take My Life	*Winston Graham*
At High Risk	*Palma Harcourt*
Dance for Diplomats	*Palma Harcourt*
Count-Down	*Hartley Howard*
The Appleby File	*Michael Innes*
A Connoisseur's Case	*Michael Innes*
Deadline for a Dream	*Bill Knox*
Death Department	*Bill Knox*
Hellspout	*Bill Knox*
The Taste of Proof	*Bill Knox*
The Affacombe Affair	*Elizabeth Lemarchand*
Let or Hindrance	*Elizabeth Lemarchand*
Unhappy Returns	*Elizabeth Lemarchand*
Waxwork	*Peter Lovesey*
Gideon's Drive	*J. J. Marric*
Gideon's Force	*J. J. Marric*
Gideon's Press	*J. J. Marric*
City of Gold and Shadows	*Ellis Peters*
Death to the Landlords!	*Ellis Peters*
Find a Crooked Sixpence	*Estelle Thompson*
A Mischief Past	*Estelle Thompson*